The
Mysterious
Mr. Ross

OTHER YEARLING BOOKS YOU WILL ENJOY:

THE MONSTER GARDEN, *Vivien Alcock*
THE STONEWALKERS, *Vivien Alcock*
THE SYLVIA GAME, *Vivien Alcock*
TRAVELERS BY NIGHT, *Vivien Alcock*
THE HAUNTING OF CASSIE PALMER, *Vivien Alcock*
DEVIL-IN-THE-FOG, *Leon Garfield*
FOOTSTEPS, *Leon Garfield*
THE NIGHT OF THE COMET, *Leon Garfield*
THE MOFFATS, *Eleanor Estes*
THE MIDDLE MOFFAT, *Eleanor Estes*

YEARLING BOOKS/YOUNG YEARLINGS/YEARLING CLASSICS are designed especially to entertain and enlighten young people. Patricia Reilly Giff, consultant to this series, received the bachelor's degree from Marymount College. She holds the master's degree in history from St. John's University, and a Professional Diploma in Reading from Hofstra University. She was a teacher and reading consultant for many years, and is the author of numerous books for young readers.

For a complete listing of all Yearling titles, write to
Dell Readers Service, P.O. Box 1045,
South Holland, IL 60473.

The Mysterious Mr. Ross

VIVIEN ALCOCK

A YEARLING BOOK

Published by
Dell Publishing
a division of
Bantam Doubleday Dell Publishing Group, Inc.
666 Fifth Avenue
New York, New York 10103

This work was first published in hardcover in Great Britain by
Methuen Children's Books Ltd.

ISBN: 0-440-40282-4

Reprinted by arrangement with Delacorte Press

Printed in the United States of America

April 1990

10 9 8 7 6 5 4 3 2 1

OPM

to Leon

*The
Mysterious
        Mr. Ross*

Chapter 1

In a way, a man's life depended on the china horse. Or at least on the breaking of the china horse.

It was Felicity Tait who broke it. Who else? She was a thin, dreamy girl who had grown suddenly so tall that she no longer seemed to know what her hands and feet were doing. Wherever she walked, small tables rocked and vases tottered. Whatever she picked up, slid through her butter fingers and shattered. She did more damage, her mother thought bitterly, than all the visitors' children together.

The Taits owned the Fairweather Guest House in Gull Bay, a shabby, rambling building facing the sea. It had once been painted bright pink, with a yellow front door, but the color had soon faded in the salt air and sharp sunlight. Now, on a dark, dismal afternoon in August, it looked like the ghost of its former self. The paint was fading and peeling. The carpets were threadbare and the sofas sagged.

And the little china horse, the one, bright, shining,

perfect thing that Mrs. Tait had possessed, lay in pieces at her feet.

"I'm sorry, Mum," Felicity said.

She knew her mother would not shout at her. Mrs. Tait never shouted at her daughters in case the guests overheard. Years of sharing her house with strangers had given her a quiet, controlled voice. Even here, in her private sitting room, she did not feel safe from listening ears.

But it was amazing how nasty she could be in a whisper.

"I was very fond of that horse," she said softly as Felicity knelt to pick up the pieces.

"Sorry, Mum."

"My grandmother gave it to me before she died. I've always treasured it."

"Sorry."

"Saying sorry's not good enough. Saying sorry won't mend my little horse, will it?"

Felicity thought of suggesting glue but decided against it.

"I didn't do it on purpose," she muttered.

"You never do. Do you realize that's the third thing you've broken this week? I sometimes wonder if there's something wrong with you."

Felicity was silent. She heard a slight rustle as her father hid behind his newspaper. Her sister was crouching over a book on the floor. Against the brown carpet, Susan looked like a plump brown rabbit pretending to be invisible. Mummy's pet knew when to keep quiet.

Her mother's voice was going on. "You know you

were forbidden to touch anything on that shelf . . . clumsy . . . careless . . . thoughtless . . ."

Felicity looked out of the window. The rain had stopped, though water still dripped down from the gutters. Their cat, Fiddles, was mincing along the top of the wall that separated the Fairweather Guest House from the Horizon Hotel next door. Every now and then he stopped to shake a wet paw fastidiously. He was a dainty cat. He never broke anything.

"Felicity, are you listening to me?" Mrs. Tait asked.

"Yes, Mum."

"Then why don't you answer me?"

Answer? Had she asked a question, then? Felicity glanced at her father for help, but he was still hidden behind his newspaper. Susan looked up from her book and mouthed something behind their mother's back. Felicity could not make it out.

"I'm waiting, Felicity," Mrs. Tait said.

Felicity could only think of one thing to do. Lose her temper.

"You're always on at me," she said furiously. "I can't do anything right. It's not fair!" She noticed that she was hissing rather than shouting the words and wished she had the courage to scream at the top of her voice. Let the guests hear. What did she care?

"I'm going out," she said.

Nobody begged her to stay. Nobody reminded her that supper was in half an hour. Susan said nothing. She was being invisible again. Her father glanced out of the window and said, as impersonally as a weatherman, that it had stopped raining. Her mother told her not to slam the door, some of the guests might be resting.

"Don't talk to strange men," she said, "And remember, you're not to go anywhere near the Gray Gulls."

Gull Bay was deserted. Heavy clouds and a pushing wind had driven even the hardiest of the summer visitors back to their hotels and boardinghouses, to shake the wet sand from their wet clothes and get ready for their evening meal. There was no one on the cold, gray beach except Felicity.

She was walking on the very edge of the sea, staring down at her bare feet as if they were some new and surprising type of fish. Beneath the curdled foam, they looked disconnected from her thin ankles, as if at any moment they might swim away and never be seen again. Gradually her face, which had been frowning, became peacefully blank.

Left, right . . . *squidge, squelch* . . . left, right.

She was trying to walk with one foot in the water and one on the wet sand, but the waves defeated her, rushing in sideways and splashing against her legs. The tide had turned.

She began running toward the West Cliff. Her feet, smashing into the water, were no longer fish but gulls diving. She mimicked their shrill cries, flapping her arms like wings.

Somebody laughed.

She looked up.

A small boy was standing on the rocks at the foot of the cliffs, a few feet beyond the warning notice. He was holding a fishnet in one hand and a red plastic bucket in the other, and was obviously a summer visitor, for he had a pale, sharp, city face and was wearing grubby sneakers on his feet.

"Me bruvver can do a better aeroplane," he said, jeering, "and he's only five."

Felicity flushed, furious at having been caught behaving like an idiot.

"What are you doing here?" she demanded, stepping up beside him, "You're not allowed past that notice board. Can't you read? Look! D-A-N-G-E-R. Danger, see? D'you want to get into trouble?"

She looked so tall and fierce that the boy backed away, gazing up at her sulkily from beneath his pale lashes. "I c'n swim," he muttered.

"I saw a drowned man once," she said, trying to frighten him, "He could swim, too, but it didn't help him. The crabs had been at him, and his eyes were gone—" It wasn't true. All she had seen, in fact, was a man being carried over the rocks in the distance. Her mother, hurrying her away, had told her that he must have fainted. It was only the next day that she had found out from her friends that it had been the body of a man who had drowned.

"There's a dangerous current out by the Gray Gulls," she warned him, adding, as he squinted at the sky, "Not those up there. *Those!*" She pointed to a line of huge, humped rocks in the distance that ran out to sea like giant stepping-stones. "They're the Gray Gulls."

"I wasn't nowhere near them. I bin here all the time,"

the boy protested. "I got as much right here as you have, anyway. 'Oo d'you think you are?"

"The coastguardsman's daughter," Felicity said, lying. "What's your name? Where are you staying?"

That frightened him. He turned, scrambled off the rocks, and went running across the sands to the seawall, pausing only to shout something, probably rude, that the wind carried away from her.

"Look out the Gulls don't get you!" she shouted back, and smiled, feeling pleased with herself. Now the bay was all hers.

She had not intended to go farther out. The wind would be colder beyond the protection of the cliffs, and the tide was coming in. Dark clouds had swallowed the sky, and it was going to rain at any moment. But something seemed to be driving her on, as if fate wanted her in a certain place at a certain time.

The rocks were partly covered with seaweed, and dotted here and there with anemones, like lumps of blood-red jelly. She began jumping idly from one to another. Her feet, hardened from years of running over sand and rock, were as sure as a cat's. She was never clumsy here. This rough shore was her element, her true home. Here there was nobody to make her nervous. Nothing to break, except her own bones, and she never thought of that. In the pools, small fish darted to hide under the seaweed as she passed by.

Picking up a long, tough piece of driftwood, she climbed up onto a flat ledge and walked along it, tapping her stick against the cliff. The ledge led gently upward, and she followed it until her way was blocked by an old rockfall, the large, tumbled boulders descending into the sea like a rough staircase. She climbed to the top and sat, her legs dangling, looking down the other side.

The narrow channel between her and the Gray Gulls was already full of jostling water. Waves rushed by and shattered against the cliff, pouring noisily into hidden crevices and dark holes. Driven by devils, as her grandmother had said.

She had brought Felicity here once. "Look down. I want you to remember this," she'd told her, pointing to the wild water. "The man you saw carried over the beach, he drowned here. The current's too strong for any swimmer, and don't you forget it. This rockfall, the sea did it. It's eating away the cliffs—see how they hang out over our heads! There'll be another fall one day. Take care you're not under it. This is the real sea, Felicity, not that tepid bathwater in the bay. Never trust it. Keep away from the Gray Gulls. I want you to promise me you won't come here again."

Felicity had promised—and broken her promise. She and her friends often came to the gully when the tide was out, looking for fossils and gemstones and jetsam from the sea. But they were always careful. They kept an eye on the sea and never let it come too close. . . .

She shivered. It was time for her to go. The wind blew colder now, and she felt a drop of rain. She looked once more into the gully.

A dark figure, wreathed in spray, had appeared out of nowhere. At first, cloaked by the shimmering drops, it seemed to be standing on the sea itself. Then the spray

fell and she saw it was a man standing on a rock. He
was dressed in a neat navy-blue suit and carried a small
case in one hand. With the waves rushing and leaping
all about him, he stood as calmly on his slippery plat-
form as if he were waiting for a suburban train.

He was a young man, with blown hair so pale that it
looked almost silver. His eyes were bright and round,
like those of a bird. He put his case down and smiled at
her. He had a surprising smile—like sunlight on a dull
day. He looked so happy that she could have cried,
knowing the danger he was in.

"Hullo," he called out above the noise of the sea.
"Silly of me. I seem to have got cut off by the tide."

Then he began to roll his trousers up to the knee.

He was going to try to wade across. He'd never make
it! He'd drown!

Chapter 2

At first Felicity could only stare at him. He looked so out of place in his city clothes. His shoes, placed neatly side by side, belonged under a bed, not on a gray rock in a wild sea. Behind him, dark clouds made a false midnight of the summer evening.

"Hey," she shouted, finding her voice at last, "you can't cross here. It's dangerous."

The wind, blowing in from the sea, snatched the words out of her mouth and wasted them on the cliffs behind her. The man looked up, but he could not have understood, for he smiled and waved. He was sitting on his rock now, dangling legs as pale as bean sprouts.

Felicity began to scramble down the rockfall. She did not stop to think about it: Thinking only made her nervous. Her hands and feet were best left to choose their own way.

Now she was level with the stranger and so close that had their arms been twice as long as they were, they might have shaken hands across the narrow channel.

The noise of rushing water was louder down here, and spray shimmered in the air between them.

"Hullo," the man called, his voice carrying faintly above the slap and gurgle of the sea. "I'm going to get my feet wet, aren't I?"

"*Don't cross here!*" she shouted as loudly as she could. "*There's a dangerous current!*"

This time he heard. He stared at her, then looked down at the swirling water.

"It doesn't look very deep," he called back, "though it's hard to tell, isn't it? If only it would keep still," he added plaintively, as a wave rushed past and burst against the cliff. He still seemed no more than mildly concerned, as if all he had to fear was a ducking.

"*You'd drown! It's the current! Even swimmers drown here!*"

"You're joking, aren't you?"

"*No! Go back! Go back the way you came!*"

The man glanced over his shoulder. "I can't!" he cried, his voice as shrill as a gull's, "I can't go back. It's even worse behind me now. There's water everywhere!"

A large wave hit the rock on which he sat, and he disappeared behind curtains of foam. When he became visible again, his face was white. He was staring down at the water. Something small and dark surfaced for a moment, then disappeared.

It was a shoe. His shoes were no longer there.

"What shall I do?" the man cried helplessly. "I can't stay here, can I? I'll have to chance it."

"*No!*" she shouted. "*Wait!*"

She tried to think. There was no time to fetch help.

The tide was coming in fast, smashing its way through the narrow gully. Already waves licked at the rocks on which they sat. Too far for him to jump. If only she had a rope . . . Then she remembered the long stick of driftwood.

"*Wait there!*" she shouted. "*I'll be back!*"

She had left the stick at the top of the rockfall and was terrified that it might have blown away. But it was still there. Snatching it up, she clambered quickly down again, hampered by having only one hand free.

The man watched her anxiously.

"Be careful!" he shouted suddenly, startling her.

Her feet shot out. She slithered helplessly to the bottom, bumping and scraping herself painfully on the way and only managing to save herself from falling into the gully by clutching a sharp knob of rock at the very last moment.

"Are you all right?" the man called.

"No thanks to you," she muttered angrily.

"What?"

"*Yes! Listen! Wait till I tell you, then jump! Catch hold of this stick! Right?*"

"Yes."

She looked down into the gully and watched a wave rush past, tearing itself into white tatters in its mad determination to batter its head against the cliff. Then the sea drew in its bubbling breath for another attack. When she could see the stones at the bottom quite plainly, she leaned right out over the gully, holding the stick out with her free hand.

"*Now!*" she shouted.

He leapt down into the water, his arm outstretched. The wood jerked wildly in her hand as he clung to it, trying to save his feet from the snatch of the sea. He was coming toward her now, teetering over the submerged stones. The stick twisted in her hand like a living thing. He was nearly there. He was smiling. . . .

A wave slapped him and he fell.

There was one last terrible pull on her arms. A sharp crack. Then nothing. The sea's roar died down to a gurgling whimper as it retreated again. She had fallen back against the rock to which she still clung with one hand. In the other was a broken piece of wood. The man had gone.

He's drowned, she thought. He's drowned.

Then she saw fingers, pale as bone, clutching the edge of the dark stone by her feet. He began to pull himself up, a glistening figure, his sodden clothes sequined with water, his hair plastered to his head.

She caught hold of his arm and tugged, and then he was flat on the rock, coughing and gasping for breath, as another wave rushed harmlessly past.

"Hurry! We're not safe yet. Come on, up there."

"I can't."

"*You've got to!*" she shouted.

Then they had no breath for talking. Only when at last they were sitting on top of the rockfall, shivering and clinging together, did they begin to chatter, on and on, as if the sea had wound up their tongues.

"My feet shot away. They simply shot away!"

"I couldn't see you. I thought you'd drowned."

"It's the end, I thought. I'm done for."

"Then I saw your hand—"

"Those rocks— Is that blood on my face, or water?"

"Water, I think."

"You saved my life," the man said. There seemed to be tears in his eyes, or perhaps they were still wet from the sea.

"But the stick broke," she said.

"You saved my life, you saved my life," he insisted. "I shall always remember."

Felicity mumbled something, embarrassed. She knew that later, back in her room, she would treasure the man's words, repeating them over and over to herself like a miser counting gold. Now she was too cold and weary to enjoy them. Her arms ached and her hands hurt. *I'm a hero*, she told herself, but could not make the angry roar of the sea sound like applause.

"I thought they'd got you," she muttered.

"Who?" the man asked, puzzled.

"Them," she said, pointing.

They looked back over the gully to where the Gray Gulls showed dimly against the overcast sky. The five huge, humped shapes seemed to be floating on the sea, with spray rising up their sides like the flutter of white wings. She shivered and turned away.

"Come on," she said. "We'd better get back. The tide's still coming in."

A cold wind blew, and gulls screamed overhead. Felicity, supporting the man from the sea, staggered forward. In the gloomy twilight they looked like a monster with two heads, lurching slowly down the wide ledge toward the quiet bay.

The man had hurt his ankle jumping down from the big rock.

"Can you help me?" he had begged. "Please? I don't want to stay here. I don't like this place very much." Though he'd smiled as he said this, his eyes had been frightened, as if he were afraid that she would run off and leave him.

It would have been more sensible if I had gone for help, Felicity thought, feeling his arm like an iron yoke across her shoulders, and a chill seeping out from his wet clothes into her side. She was dazed with exhaustion. Her ear, flattened against his chest, seemed to hear a dull roar, like the sound of the sea in a shell. Often she had an illusion that she was carrying the man on her back, a dead weight, heavy and cold. She was surprised, looking sideways, to see him limping and hopping beside her.

Their tired feet slipped and stumbled over the damp rock, and once he tripped, nearly bringing them both down.

"I'm too heavy for you," he said. But he did not let her go.

They were back in the bay now, out of the worst of the wind. Felicity looked across to the town. The lights were on, but there was no one in sight. It was raining, a thin, silver rain stitching the sea to the wet sky, as if to enclose the whole world with water. She saw with pleasure that the tide had nearly reached the steps in the seawall.

"We can swim from here," she said as the man exclaimed in alarm, seeing the rock ledge that led straight down into the sea. "It's not rough in the bay. The waves will carry us in. Easier than walking."

"I can't swim," he said.

She stared at him. Then she said, trying not to let her weariness sound in her voice, "That's all right. Just lie flat on your back and I'll tow you in. I'm a good swimmer. I've got medals."

She looked at the row of buildings on the rising ground above the shore. She could see the lights of the Fairweather Guest House shining through the rain, and wondered if the guests were making the same old jokes about its name, the jokes they made every wet summer. It was too far to see if anyone was standing on the front steps, looking out for her. She sighed, wishing someone would come and fetch them in a boat.

The man was watching her. "You're tired," he said gently, "And cold. You've done too much for me. You'd better go on alone—"

"And leave you here? Of course I won't! Don't worry. I'll get you home safe."

She did her best. She got him as far as the pebbles by the seawall. At first, coming out of the shallow rim of the sea, he tried to help, floundering on the wet stones, pushing himself over the last inches to safety. Then he collapsed. He lay facedown, coughing and retching, and would not answer her. He shuddered, gasped several times, and lay still.

Chapter 3

There was no one in sight. Felicity stumbled across the road, screaming at the top of her voice.

"Dad! Dad! Dad!"

The sound bounced off the wet walls of the buildings opposite and echoed down the empty promenade, until she sounded like a thousand gulls crying.

The front door of the Fairweather Guest House opened, and she saw her mother silhouetted against the light, her shadow lying on the steps like a narrow black carpet. Behind her, the guests were spilling out of their lounge, pink faces staring.

Then she was in the hall and her mother was holding her, asking her questions. They were all asking questions, crowding so close that she felt she could not breathe. The sound of the sea still roared in her ears.

"She's going to faint," someone said.

Hands held her, hands moved her, pushed her down —she was sitting on the stairs with her head hanging forward over her knees. Her mother was saying, "Take three deep breaths, Felicity—"

"Where's Dad? I want Dad!"

"He's not here. He's out looking for you. It's all right, dear. Mummy's here. Everything's all right now."

Stupid. Everything was *not* all right. She had to tell them . . . the man . . .

"You've got to help," she said breathlessly. "Somebody's got to help. He's too heavy for me. I can't . . . I can't . . ."

"Who's too heavy?" her mother asked sharply. "Felicity, has there been an accident?"

An accident? Felicity was confused. It had not seemed like an accident, she thought, remembering the cold fury of the wave knocking the man down. The sea had done it on purpose, she was sure of that. . . .

"Never trust it," her grandmother had told her.

"*Felicity!*" Her mother was shaking her. "Felicity, pull yourself together. What's happened? *Tell me!*"

Felicity's head cleared. She saw her mother's face, very close, looking enormously worried. She heard her sister's voice saying, "It's not Dad, is it? Has something happened to Dad?"

"No! No, not Dad. It's—I don't know who it is—a stranger," she said, and saw the relief in her mother's face. She tried to tell them what had happened, but her words tumbled out in such confusion that at first they did not understand her. "Somebody's got to help," she kept saying. "He's just lying there and he won't get up. I didn't hold his head under the water. I know I didn't—"

They all stared at her in horrified bewilderment. All except Susan.

"Mum, she's been playing by the Gulls again," her sister said. "And somebody's got drowned."

"He hasn't! He hasn't! You can't cough when you're dead, can you? Can you, Mum?"

"No, of course not," her mother said briskly. "Where's this man now?"

"On the beach. By the steps. I'll show you."

She tried to stand up, but her mother pushed her down again as easily as if she were a rag doll.

"No, dear. You rest here a minute. Don't worry. We'll find him. Susan, fetch some towels from the airing cupboard. And blankets! Did you hear me, Susan? Now, if some of you men will come with me—"

"I'm coming! I want to come!" Felicity cried, trying to stand up, but her legs were as weak and wobbly as string. She sat down with a jolt and leaned her spinning head against the banisters.

Dimly she heard voices and footsteps receding. Someone brushed past her, and her sister said, "Where am I supposed to put these? Are they for her?"

A blanket was thrown around Felicity's shoulders, and something soft was dumped beside her on the stairs. She opened her eyes and saw Susan hurrying away across the hall.

"Wait for me!" she cried, "Susan, wait for me!"

But Susan had already run out into the rain, and Felicity was still too dizzy to follow her. Through the open door she could see the guests hurrying across the road. Some had gone out as they were. Others had stopped long enough to put on raincoats. Two small boys were being chased by a fat woman with an umbrella.

They'd left her behind. They'd gone off without her, all of them, even her mother. A half-drowned stranger was more exciting than a bruised and exhausted daughter. She could be dying for all they'd care, she thought angrily, picking at a deep scratch on her leg, trying to make it bleed again.

"It's not fair," she muttered, and began to cry.

Somebody sighed and said, "Now what am I supposed to do?"

Felicity was startled, for she had thought she was alone in the hall. One of the guests must have stayed behind. She kept her face hidden in her hands and hoped the woman, whoever she was, would go away.

There was a pause, then the woman said, "Do you think you could stop crying for a minute? It makes conversation a bit difficult."

Felicity recognized the voice now. It belonged to Miss Pepper, the last person you'd want to see when your face was blotched with tears and your nose running. Miss Pepper, who had booked their very best room for six weeks—first-floor double with its own bath and a view of the sea. Miss Pepper, who walked coolly through the shabby rooms, leaving a wake of curious whispers behind her wherever she went.

She seemed out of place at the Fairweather. Too posh, as Susan said. Too well dressed. She never strolled along the shore or went bathing or bought a picture postcard. She just sat on the veranda all day with a book she never read, gazing out to sea.

"Probably wondering why on earth she came here," Susan had said. "She looks as if she'd be more at home in Monte Carlo. I know—she's lost all her money gambling and she's waiting for the sea to warm up before she throws herself in. I hope she remembers to pay her bill first."

Felicity was more romantic. "She's waiting for her lover. He's a sailor and she's watching for his ship to come in. Nobody's dared tell her it's been wrecked and her lover is at the bottom of the sea. She'll go on waiting and waiting until her red hair turns as white as his bones—"

"Good. Then Mum will have a permanent lodger, and we'll make a lot of money out of her."

Felicity had laughed at this, but now, looking at Miss Pepper, she wondered if she had been right, after all. There was a feeling of weary patience about the woman, as if she were waiting for something that was taking too long to come. Her face was pale and slightly haggard. Her diamond earrings seemed to spit coldly against her red hair, like snowflakes on fire.

The man from the sea! Felicity thought. It must be him! He's come back to her at last. . . . She looks too old for him.

Miss Pepper, unaware of this last unflattering thought, smiled down at her.

"That's better," she said. "Now. A hot bath and then bed. Don't you think that would be a good idea?"

"No."

"Some peroxide in the water for those scratches," the woman went on, as if Felicity had not spoken.

Felicity did not want a bath. "The sea has iodine in it," she said.

"So it has. All right. You can have some of my new bath oil instead. French. Very expensive. Made out of lemon flowers and . . . skunk, I believe they use."

"Skunk?"

"It doesn't sound likely, I agree. Perhaps I've got it wrong," the woman said, sounding bored. "Run along and have your bath, there's a good girl."

"I don't need a bath. I'm clean."

"Well, for heaven's sake, go and put your dressing gown on and pretend you've had a bath," Miss Pepper said, adding, as Felicity stared at her in surprise, "Your mother told me to see to it. Apparently everyone is expected to help in an emergency, and I got landed with you. I was the only one left. All the others ran out to watch. Little did I think when I came here that I'd be expected to look after a child. I'm not very good with children. I'm not used to them. Are you going to have your bath, or am I supposed to offer you a bribe? Is that what you're waiting for?"

"No!" Felicity said indignantly, though she could not help wondering how much it would have been. "My room's right up in the attic," she explained. "And my legs feel funny. And I haven't had any supper. And I want to see the man brought in."

"Oh, dear," the woman said, and sighed. "Do you have to be so difficult? Look, my room's on the first floor. Room three. My bathrobe's behind the door. Can you manage to get it, or am I expected to carry you up? No? Good. Here's my key. You'll have plenty of time if you hurry." She looked through the open front door. A cluster of women stood at the top of the steps in the seawall, gazing down. "There's nothing happening yet," she said. "Look at them, just standing there getting wet. What good do they think they're doing? They'll only be in the way. Like a silly flock of sheep. We don't want to join them, do we?" she added with such an air of mutual superiority that Felicity, who did want to, weakly said, "No."

"Run along, then," Miss Pepper said.

Felicity limped up the stairs. At the top she turned and looked down. Miss Pepper was now standing by the front door, staring out into the rain.

She's just as curious as all the others, Felicity thought, only she doesn't want to get wet. Susan says she dyes her hair. Perhaps she's afraid the color will run. She doesn't want the man to see her looking like a vampire, with red streaks trickling down her chin like blood. He might not love her anymore. If he really is the one she's been waiting for . . .

It'd be one in the eye for Susan if he were. Susan always said the stories Felicity made up about the guests were silly: "It's all that junk you read. Shipwrecked twins and haunted abbeys and mixed-up love potions indeed! It's all rot. Life isn't like that!" Susan was three years older than Felicity and always behaved as if her extra time on earth had been spent in a serious study of mankind instead of drooling in her baby carriage.

It wasn't, of course, but it ought to be, Felicity thought. If only she could prove her sister wrong. But she was not certain if she really wanted the man to be claimed by Miss Pepper. Miss Pepper had not been very nice to her. She did not deservé a happy ending.

Besides, she thought, *I saved his life. In a way, that makes him mine. He belongs to me, not to anybody else.*

Chapter 4

Now the hall was full of glistening people, plastic rain-coats, and dripping umbrellas. Wet footprints confused the pattern of the carpet.

"Here he comes," Miss Pepper said.

She and Felicity were on the first-floor landing, look-ing down over the banisters, when the man was carried in through the front door. A folded deck chair was be-ing used as a stretcher. It was too short. His bare legs dangled awkwardly over the edge, as thin and limp as empty stockings. His face was pale, the line of small bruises on his cheekbone showing up like dirty finger-prints on clean china. His mouth was open.

Felicity glanced quickly at the woman beside her, but Miss Pepper's face showed no sign of recognition. She might have been a housewife looking down at a sole on a fishmonger's slab, wondering whether to have it for her dinner. Deciding it wasn't worth the price.

"He looks different when he's dry," Felicity said de-fensively. "More . . . well . . ." But she could not find words to describe the impression he'd made on her. "Nicer," she ended weakly.

Miss Pepper looked amused. "I hope you're not disappointed in him. It's too late to throw him back in the sea. I suppose that's one of the risks of saving someone's life. You don't know what you're getting. He might turn out to be . . ."

"To be what?"

"Oh, I don't know. Anyone. Anything."

"Everybody's worth saving," Felicity said hotly, and Miss Pepper laughed.

"You sound like a Baptist preacher," she said, "I wonder if you're right. I can think of people I wouldn't lift a finger to save."

"Who?" Felicity asked curiously, but Miss Pepper only smiled and went into her room, shutting the door behind her.

Felicity frowned. Then she shrugged and, holding up the skirts of her borrowed bathrobe, went slowly down the stairs.

There was an extension at the back of the Fairweather Guest House, a small room built of brick with a square window and a door opening onto the garden. It had been intended as storage for garden chairs in winter and wet weather, but when Grandmother Tait could no longer manage the stairs, it had been made into a bedroom for her, and the chairs were moved to a wooden shed at the bottom of the garden. After her death it had remained empty, except for an occasional aunt or cousin, visiting when the guest house was full.

It was here they put the man from the sea. There had been talk of ringing for an ambulance and sending him to the hospital, but one of the guests, Miss Tatterson from Room 7, was a nurse. She said there was nothing much wrong with him, except a sprained ankle and exhaustion. She could bandage the one, and a good night's sleep would deal with the other.

"Send for a doctor by all means, if you really think it necessary," she'd said, making it quite clear that she did not.

The stranger lay in Gran's old bed, as docile as a sleepy child. He drank his hot milk. He smiled. He thanked everybody in a weak, almost inaudible voice.

When they asked him if anybody was expecting him, if there was anyone he'd like them to get in touch with, he shook his head.

"Are you sure?" Mrs. Tait asked. "What about your family? Your friends?"

"No," he said, "There's no one."

When they asked him his name, they thought at first he had not heard, for he did not answer. His eyes, glancing vaguely past them, were as unfocused as a baby's. There was something oddly appealing about his helplessness. He made them feel strong and kind.

"Poor man, let him sleep now," Miss Tatterson said. "You can find out in the morning."

But as they reached the door they heard him say, "Albert Ross."

They looked back. His face was turned into the pillow. It was almost as if he'd spoken in his sleep. They closed the door quietly behind them.

The man moved his head. He gazed slowly around, noticing everything, taking possession of the room with his eyes. A small table by the window; a wooden chair, painted white; a framed chart of seabirds on the wall; a green carpet on the floor—all dimly seen in the partial darkness, like things under water. He smiled. Then, turning to face the wall, he went to sleep, curled up like a child.

Felicity had not seen the man put to bed. Her father was back, and he had taken her into the kitchen, where Susan was heating up her supper.

She sat in a happy daze, spooning up chicken soup with an unsteady hand. Little yellow drops freckled the front of Miss Pepper's bathrobe. But nobody told her off. Her bowl was taken away, the soup poured into a mug and handed back to her.

"There, that's better, isn't it?" her father asked. "Poor Fliss. You can hardly keep your eyes open, can you? You ought to be in bed."

"I'm not tired," Felicity protested.

It wasn't true. Waves of sleep kept threatening to engulf her. It was as if the sea had gotten into her head, a gentle, rocking sea in which smiling faces swam before her eyes.

This was her night of triumph. She was determined not to miss a moment of it, even if she had to hold her eyelids apart with her fingers. The kitchen was warm with admiration, the smell of soup, and a faint, lingering whiff of antiseptic. Miss Tatterson had come looking for more work, and Felicity's right hand, badly grazed and swollen, was now covered with a large white bandage, guaranteed to catch every eye.

"You poor dear, it must be very painful."

"Aren't you a brave girl!"

"She deserves a medal."

"Yes, indeed."

The guests, made restive by the excitement, kept coming into the kitchen for hot drinks, and they all made a fuss over her, wanting to hear about the rescue.

It was her mother's face she watched. A little anxiously. Her mother was being very kind. She had fetched a cushion when she noticed Felicity wriggling her bruised shoulders against the hard back of the chair. Her voice was gentle and her smiles frequent, switching on and off like the lights of a Christmas tree. But between the smiles, her face looked very grave, and she called Felicity "dear" so often and so pointedly that Felicity began to feel like a luxury her mother could not afford.

Perhaps she was merely worrying about the milk running out, with so many requests for coffee and hot chocolate. Or perhaps she was remembering that Felicity had promised never to go out to the Gray Gulls and was wondering how to tell her off when everyone else was praising her.

It was so unfair, Felicity thought. All her friends went to the gully when the tide was out. If she stopped going, she'd lose them. They wouldn't mean to be horrid. They'd just forget to tell her things, leave her out of their plans, might not even notice that she wasn't there.

Her mother just didn't understand. It was perfectly

safe in the gully if you kept an eye on the sea. They weren't fools, playing last-across like babies. They were serious collectors. They knew all about times and tides and in fact were in less danger than many a summer visitor heading out to sea on a float in the deceptive safety of the bay, with an offshore wind blowing them halfway to France and a gale warning ruffling the edges of the sky.

But just try telling her mother that! Mum didn't like the sea. It was just something to get the guests out of her way for a few hours. And she positively hated sand. Sand to her was just so much dirt, a nasty, sharp yellow dust that got into everything on purpose to annoy. It blocked the vacuum cleaner, lay like grit in the bottom of baths, scratched the tiles, and somehow, however careful she was, got into the food.

"For heaven's sake, shake yourself before you come in," she was always telling Felicity. "You're covered in sand. You must roll in it. Susan never gets herself into such a mess."

Susan never played on the beach nowadays. She just lay on a towel, turning herself like a sausage on a grid. Or hung round the amusement arcade with her friends, giggling at the boys. But Felicity did not tell her mother that. Susan might retaliate, and there were too many things Felicity did not want Mum to know. Such as the question old Miss Vincent from Room 2 was asking now—

"But I thought the bay was safe. That's what it said in the brochure. Safe bathing."

"Yes. Yes, it is," Felicity said, conscious that her

mother was listening. "He was right out by the Gray Gulls. Wasn't it lucky I heard him? I'd never have known he was out there if he hadn't shouted for help."

"Where were you?" Mrs. Tait asked.

"I was paddling in the bay," Felicity replied, looking her mother straight in the eye. Then, remembering having read somewhere that this was what hardened liars did, she glanced quickly away. "I thought he was some sort of great gull at first. Then I heard it more clearly: 'Help! Help! Save me! Won't anybody save me!' " She saw from Susan's warning frown that she was overdoing it and added hastily, "Or something like that. I couldn't really make out the exact words."

To her relief her mother accepted this, and although she said that Felicity should have fetched help instead of trying to do it all by herself, she did not seem cross.

"I expect you didn't stop to think," she said quite kindly. "You never do. But another time, run for help. It was lucky both you and Mr. Ross weren't drowned. You might easily have been."

"Mr. Ross? Is that his name?"

"Yes, dear. Albert Ross."

"Albert! Yuk!" Susan said, screwing up her nose, "What a horrible name. He doesn't look like an Albert."

"What does an Albert look like?" someone asked.

Felicity heard their voices dimly. She was suddenly, overwhelmingly tired. Her legs ached. Her hand hurt. She seemed to feel again the cold weight of the man's arm across her shoulders, and a sharp wind blowing. Her eyes closed, and immediately her mind was filled with strange pictures, pictures of a doomed ship on a burning sea, of fire and ice and a dead white bird. They were oddly familiar. She had seen them somewhere before.

Chapter 5

That night Felicity dreamed she was fishing. There was something caught in her net. "Throw it back!" Miss Pepper screamed. "Throw it back before it's too late! Throw it! Throw it!"

It was only the morning gulls, screeching like alarm clocks above her attic room. She sat up, knowing it was not their noise that had awakened her. She was too used to it. It was something else. Something she had wanted to do.

The house was quiet. No sound of traffic, no whine of a milk truck on the road outside. The air had that fresh, sharp, unused feeling, and the sky outside her window was hazily bright. It was going to be a fine day.

But when? She looked at her watch. Shook it. Hit it. It was no good. The salt water had ruined it. Shrugging, she got out of bed, dressed quickly, and crept down through the sleeping house.

The clock on the kitchen wall said ten past six. Too early. She put the kettle on and laid the tray, then sat

and watched the minute hand jerk and doze its way
down the face of the clock until she could bear it no
longer. She hated waiting; it made her nervous. Perhaps
his watch had stopped, too, and he would not realize
how early it was.

At half past six she was in the garden, the tray in her
hands, standing outside the stranger's door. In the trees
the birds chattered in alarm, warning each other of a
danger she could not see. From the garden room there
was no sound at all.

"Mr. Ross?" she called softly.

No answer.

"Mr. Ross!" she called loudly.

Silence.

What was the matter with him? Didn't he know his
own name? Or had he made off in the night, vanishing
as quickly as he had appeared?

Balancing the tray awkwardly against her hip, she
knocked, opened the door, and went in.

"Wha-what? Who's that? Who is it?"

"Me. I've brought you some tea. I did knock."

He was lying in bed, his head turned toward her. His
eyes, wide open and as round as pennies, stared at her
blankly, as if he had no idea who she was or what she
was doing in his room. He looked, oddly, both younger
and older than she had thought. His fair hair had dried
into tangled wisps, and his borrowed pajamas hung
loosely from his thin shoulders, making him look like a
boy dressed up in his father's clothes. But the skin beneath his eyes was as gray and lined as driftwood. He
looked sickly, as if he'd been kept in a dark cupboard

too long and would never bloom. She could not help feeling disappointed.

"How are you?" she asked politely.

"The same. No better. I never seem to get any better," he said petulantly. "I'm sick and tired of being shut in here—" He broke off abruptly and stared round the room.

"I'm sorry," she mumbled, not knowing what she was apologizing for. Her bandaged hand made her clumsy. She put the tray down on the table with a bang that made the china rattle. A little tea belched out of the spout and stained the clean cloth.

"It's *you!*" he cried, in quite a different voice. "Of course. You're the girl who saved my life. I'm sorry. I was half asleep. For a moment I thought I was back in—" He stopped abruptly and coughed.

"Back where?" she asked curiously.

"You've hurt your hand!"

"Yes, a bit. Where did you think—"

"Did it happen last night? On the rocks? You never told me. You are brave."

Felicity, smiling and flushing, turned away to pour out his tea and quite forgot what she'd been about to ask him.

When he sat up to take the cup from her, he winced, screwing his face up like a paper bag.

"What's the matter? Is it your ankle?"

"Mmm."

"Isn't it any better?"

He shook his head. "I can hardly bear to move it. I wish I didn't feel so horribly weak. I don't think I'll be able to walk . . ." His hand shook as he put his cup down. "What am I going to do?" he asked helplessly.

"Stay in bed, I suppose," she said, as he seemed to expect an answer.

"May I really?" He lay back on his pillows and smiled. "But won't I be an awful nuisance? Are you sure your mother won't mind?"

Felicity was not at all sure.

She knew her mother was kind because everybody told her so. She did a lot of work for charities—at a distance. Mrs. Tait sat on committees, which is easier on the legs than carrying trays backward and forward. She'd had enough of that when Gran was ill. Running a guest house was hard work, without having an invalid to look after. Not that she'd ever complained. She had just bought herself some elastic stockings and suffered. But that was for Gran, not for a strange man her daughter had fished out of the sea.

I could do it, Felicity thought. *I could bring him all his meals, if only she'd trust me. But she won't. Just because I dropped that tray—I was only trying to help. How was I to know that somebody'd moved the footstool? She's always on at me. "Put that down, Felicity! Careful! Mind that vase! Look where you're going!" It's a wonder I'm not a nervous wreck. When the summer kids break anything, all she says is, "Never mind, dear. It was an accident," and down it goes on the bill. She seems to forget I pay too. She's always stopping my pocket money. . . .*

She was deep in these resentful thoughts when she realized Mr. Ross was talking to her.

"I'm sorry. What did you say?"

"I said you were all so kind. It's a great load off my mind, I can tell you, finding somewhere to stay like this. I feel quite at home here already."

Felicity looked at him blankly. He spoke as if something had been settled between them, some promise made, but she could not remember having agreed to anything. Perhaps she had moved her head up and down, not meaning yes but just because her bruised neck was stiff. Susan was right. She ought to listen more often to what people were saying. But it was usually so boring.

She tried to concentrate, but it was not easy. He had such a weak, husky voice that a bird had only to twitter in the garden to drown out several words.

He told her he had been out of England for a long, long time, but though she listened carefully, she could not make out what he had been doing, nor where exactly he had been. His failing voice and frequent coughing seemed to smooth out all hard facts. She got the impression he had been a traveler, a wanderer in faraway places. In one of them he must have been ill, because he said he had only waited to be well enough to set out for home.

"But it's all changed so much. It seems like a foreign country to me now. I've lost touch with all—" A bird sang loudly in the garden and drowned out his next words.

He cleared his throat. "—like a stranger," he went on more clearly, "cut off from—"

"You should've taken the cliff path," Felicity told him, hearing the words *cut off* and feeling herself on firm ground at last. "Or the bus. There's a good bus from Gullington. It runs every hour."

He looked somewhat surprised by this sensible advice.

"You were coming from Gullington, weren't you?" she asked.

He started coughing and did not answer.

As she waited for him to stop, she was suddenly reminded of William Bedford at school. Not that he looked like Mr. Ross. It was just having to wait in the middle of a conversation. William Bedford had hay fever, for which he took pills that did not work. In summer, almost everything made him sneeze: dust, pollen, cat's fur, chalk. The teachers had only to ask him an awkward question to bring on a fit of sneezing.

Why had she thought of that? Mr. Ross wasn't trying to avoid answering, was he?

Suddenly doubtful, she listened carefully. Last night his cough had been thick and wet, full of seawater and spit. Now it was dry, rapid, distinct. You could have written it down on paper—"Ahem, ahem, ahem." An artificial sound. A stage direction.

He was sitting up and leaning forward, one hand politely covering his mouth and the other shading his eyes. Like two thirds of the brass monkeys on her father's desk: see no evil, speak no evil. Only hear no evil was missing.

He finished coughing and lay back, looking exhausted. There was a sheen of sweat on his pale skin. He *is* ill, she thought with relief. He's not putting it on.

His eyes were looking round the room anxiously, as if searching for something.

"Mum hung your clothes up to dry," Felicity said quickly, to reassure him. "It's all right. Your money was still in your pockets. Mum spread the notes out on a towel, and your loose change is in that blue-and-white jug over there. I'm afraid there was nothing else. I mean, no keys or checkbook or anything like that. They must've fallen out."

For a moment she thought he looked angry, as if he hated the idea of someone searching his pockets while he slept. Then he said it was kind of her mother to have taken so much trouble.

"My case?" he asked. "I don't remember . . . it's gone, hasn't it? It's gone."

"It must've fallen into the sea, I'm afraid."

"Then I've lost it."

"Did it have much in it?" she asked.

"Everything." He spread his thin hands dramatically, as if to show how empty they were. "Not only clothes but everything—passport, papers, letters, photographs . . . My whole life was in there."

"But it was only a small case," she said before she could stop herself. It sounded rude, though she hadn't meant it to. She was always in trouble for saying the first thing that came into her head.

To her relief he began to laugh helplessly, shaking with laughter until tears came into his eyes. Felicity began to laugh, too, though she did not know why he found it quite so funny.

"Only a small case," he said at last, wiping his eyes. "You could say that was the story of my life."

"What do you mean?"

"Oh, just that I'm such an unimportant person. A very small fish, I'm afraid," he said apologetically, as if he had guessed that she'd hoped he would turn out to be someone rich and famous.

"You're not!" she said, flushing. "I'm sure you're not. Anyway, I don't like important people. They're boring."

He smiled at her, murmured something that she did not hear, and shut his eyes. She stood looking down at him, wondering if he'd fallen asleep. She had meant to ask him a favor, but she had left it too late. She could not wake him now. People were often annoyed if you woke them up. Besides, he looked so defenseless, lying as still and gray as an effigy on a tomb.

I don't care who he is, she thought. *He is important to me. I've never saved anyone's life before. I usually break things. I hope Mum doesn't turn him out because he's ill and hasn't much money. . . .*

Her mother, going through his pockets the previous night, had seemed puzzled not to find a checkbook or credit cards.

They must have been in his case, Felicity thought. Or perhaps she said the words aloud, for Mr. Ross opened his eyes and said sleepily, "Gone."

"It might not be," Felicity said eagerly, seeing a chance to ask her favor and offer one in return. "Your case, I mean. It might've got caught in the rocks. All sorts of things do. We found a whole lot of oranges in the gully once, hundreds of them. Bony said they must've come off a ship. They tasted horrible, though. We spat them out, and Meg said we'd all die—" She saw Mr. Ross's eyes becoming glazed and was afraid that he would go back to sleep. "I could look for your case," she went on loudly. "This afternoon. At low tide."

"But . . . isn't it dangerous?"

"No. Not if you're careful. And we are, honestly. We know all about the tides. Bony White's got a great chart. I could take him with me."

"But—"

"I'd be perfectly safe," she insisted. "The only thing is . . ." She hesitated. This was the difficult part. "The thing is, Mum would only worry if she knew. She's funny that way. She worries about everything, so it's better if she doesn't know. I mean, like last night. I had to tell her I went out to the Gulls because I'd heard you shout for help."

He was silent for a long time, staring at her. She began to wish she had left it alone. Her mother had believed her and might never have thought of checking. But now—grown-ups could be difficult. They didn't want to take responsibility in case anything went wrong. Mr. Ross might think it his duty to tell her mother, and then she'd be in trouble.

"Did I shout for help?" he asked.

She was silent, not knowing how to take this.

"Last night is all confused in my mind," he said, watching her face, "I can only remember it in snatches —the sea . . . my shoes going . . . and you, the stick you held out to me, leaning so bravely over the gully. You saved my life. I will never forget that."

She flushed and looked at him doubtfully. Was it a bargain, then? Was that what he meant? He would not give her away because she had saved his life?

"How many times did I shout?" he asked. "I'd better know, hadn't I?"

"Several times. Very loudly." Felicity said happily, and they smiled at each other, the bargain sealed.

But as she was leaving the room, the tray in her hands, he sat up and said urgently, "You will be careful, won't you? Please. I'd never forgive myself if anything happened to you. Promise you'll be careful. It's a horrible place. Don't stay there too long."

"I won't," she assured him, looking back over her shoulder. "I'm always careful."

Then she tripped over the doorsill and fell out into the garden in a crash of her mother's china.

Her luck held. It was only ten past seven, and her mother was not yet up. The broken crockery, hidden at the bottom of a trash can, would probably never be missed. On her way back to her attic she met Susan coming out of her room, flushed and yawning in a flowered nightie.

"You're up early. Where have you been?" Susan asked her.

"I took Mr. Ross some tea," Felicity said. "Only don't tell Mum."

"Why not? What have you broken this time?"

"Nothing. Well, nothing much."

Susan laughed. "Come and tell me about him," she said, going back into her room. "What did you find out? I hope he's rich. What does he do? Where did he come from? Gullington? Tell me everything."

But there was very little Felicity could tell.

"He's been abroad," she said vaguely, "but he was ill, so he came back."

"What was the matter with him?"

"I don't know."

"I hope it's nothing infectious. What country was he in?"

"I don't know. All over the place, I think."

"What was he doing?"

"Sort of wandering about."

"You don't seem to have found out much," Susan complained. "You are a doze. I suppose you were day-dreaming again. You never listen to what people say."

"I do! I did! He's—he's a great explorer. He was in China, living with pandas in the bamboo forests. Getting to know them, learning their language. They have a sort of language. They're very clever animals. They looked after him when he was sick, brought him sugar-cane to suck, that sort of thing. He's going to write a book about them, and it'll make him rich and famous, and there'll be a film made—"

"And you'll go to the premiere in a golden dress and a diamond tiara. You're slipping, Fliss. That's too far-fetched, even for you. I thought you were going to claim he was Miss Pepper's lost lover. The one you say she's waiting for."

"I did think of that," Felicity admitted, "but I'm sure she didn't recognize him. I was watching her face."

"She might have been deliberately covering up. Did you think of that? They might be spies. He's probably come off a Russian submarine. I'm surprised that hasn't occurred to you. Hey, I'm not serious, you little idiot!" Susan said, seeing Felicity's eyes become thoughtful. "For heaven's sake, don't start spreading stories about him. Tell you what, I'll go and see him after breakfast. I bet I find out all there is to know about him in ten minutes flat."

I expect she will, Felicity thought, going back to her room. *And I expect it will be dull and ordinary enough. Like his name. Albert Ross.*

Albert Ross, she repeated to herself, and wondered why it echoed in her head with the wild sound of the sea and white wings beating.

Chapter 6

Her friends came after breakfast, all eager to hear about the rescue. It was the best morning of her life, and she was sorry when it was over. She stood in the doorway, looking after them until they were out of sight. Then she glanced toward the sea. Behind a frieze of summer visitors on the promenade it lay quietly, as flat as a sequined carpet spread over the bay. Innocent. Harmless.

"Never trust it," her grandmother had said. She had spoken almost as if the sea were a bad-tempered dog, capable of snapping at you if you took its bone away.

At least it's kept on a lead, Felicity thought, trying to laugh away her uneasiness. *It's got to go walkies when the moon pulls it. There's no way it can get me at low tide, even if it wants to.*

And, of course, it did not. It was silly to talk as if the sea had feelings. It was only a lot of cold water sloshing about. Nevertheless, she was glad she had asked Bony White to come with her to search the gully. He was always cautious, because he could not swim. He knew all about tides and currents and, better still, had a watch as big as an ashtray, which you could set like an alarm clock to ring a bell when it was time to go. She would be safe with Bony. He never took risks.

She turned back into the hall and saw Miss Pepper coming in from the garden, with a red rose in her hand.

"Hullo, all alone?" Miss Pepper said. "You look a little gloomy. Has your audience run out on you? Too bad. Just when you were enjoying yourself."

"They wanted to hear about it," Felicity said indignantly. "They asked me to tell them. I wasn't boasting."

"No, no. You were very modest. I heard you," Miss Pepper said soothingly. "I particularly liked the way you waved aside their compliments with your bandaged hand. Such a big bandage too! Most effective. But where are they all gone? There were at least a hundred children on the veranda an hour ago."

"There were only nine of us," Felicity said, refusing to smile. "And we offered you a seat, but you said you didn't want it."

"Children frighten me," Miss Pepper confessed. "Especially in large numbers. I hope I didn't drive them away."

"No. They've gone into Gullington for the donkey derby."

Miss Pepper laughed. "That's what I call unfair competition. Donkeys! No wonder you look disheartened. Fame doesn't last long, does it? Here, have this rose," she said, holding it out. "I'm sorry it isn't a medal."

"It's a Scarlet Glory," Felicity said coldly. "From our garden."

"I didn't steal it, I promise. Your Mr. Ross gave it to me."

"Mr. Ross? Oh." Felicity felt a pang, as sharp as a thorn. Mr. Ross had not given her a rose. She had not seen him again. When she had tried to take Susan to the garden room after breakfast, they had been shooed away by their mother and Miss Tatterson. "I'm sorry. No visitors," Miss Tatterson had said, with a smile so brisk that she should have been wearing a starched uniform to go with it. "He still needs complete quiet. The longer he can sleep, the better." And their mother, looking at them pointedly, had hung a PLEASE DO NOT DISTURB sign on the handle of his door. But apparently this only applied to children. Any aging adult with dyed red hair could walk in and out as she pleased.

"I don't want your rose," she said, handing it back. "It's got aphids on it."

"Now what have I done to upset you?" Miss Pepper asked, looking at Felicity's flushed face. "I'm sorry, whatever it is. I warned you I was no good with children. I never know how to talk to them."

"It's quite easy. Just talk to us as if we were people. We'll understand."

"Oh, dear, you are cross, aren't you? Why? Is it because Mr. Ross didn't give you a rose?"

"No! Of course it isn't!" Felicity said furiously. "I can pick all the roses I want. They're ours. I can pick every one."

"He was only being grateful," Miss Pepper said, not even trying to hide her amusement at this outburst. "He's an extremely polite young man, isn't he? Your mother took him in some coffee and biscuits on a tray, and a jugful of roses. I only held the door open for her. He seemed quite overcome with gratitude. One almost could have sworn there were tears in his eyes. He didn't know how to thank us, he said, so he gave us back a rose each. A yellow one for your mother and a red one for me. To match our hair, perhaps. Your mother thought it was a charming gesture. She seems very taken with him. Perhaps she's always wanted a son."

Felicity stared.

"You don't like him, do you?" she said slowly.

"Oh," Miss Pepper said, shrugging, "somehow I never trust charming people. I wouldn't fall in love with him if I were you."

"Of course I won't."

"How old are you? Fifteen? Sixteen? Just the age to imagine yourself in love. I did, I remember. He taught us Scripture and he looked like an angel. I would have died for him."

"I'm not silly," Felicity said with dignity. "And, anyway, I'm only twelve."

"As young as that?" Miss Pepper said, surprised. For a moment she looked disconcerted. "I thought you were older—you're so tall. You mustn't take me seriously. I like teasing people. Really, I have nothing against your Mr. Ross. I'm sure he is a perfectly respectable young man. I only wish that he didn't have such an aggravating cough." She turned and tucked the rose into a bowl of flowers on the hall table, scattering petals all over its polished surface. "There. Poor rose, nobody wants you.

I must go up and powder my nose. It must be nearly time I was going out for lunch."

With that she smiled at Felicity, wiggled her fingers in the air, and went upstairs.

For a moment Felicity stared after her. Then she looked back at the vase of flowers. Already the red rose was looking dejected. Overblown.

To match her hair, Felicity thought scornfully. Whom does she think she's kidding? If she wants to fool people, she shouldn't keep a bottle of hair dye in her bathroom.

She flicked the rose with her fingers, and it immediately shed five more petals. Smiling a little guiltily, she wondered if it would have the same effect as sticking pins in a wax effigy. Perhaps the next time Miss Pepper appeared, she would be half bald and then nobody would admire her.

The Fairweather Guest House did not do lunches. Not for the guests, that is. Mrs. Benson, who helped out every summer, prepared a meal for the family, but the guests had to go to Candy's Café on the seafront, or the Copper Kettle in the High Street, or even, if they could afford it, to sit in gloomy splendor in the Old Ship's dining room.

"That's the last of them gone," Mrs. Tait would say with relief.

With any luck they would not be back until it was time for their evening meal, and for five or six blessed hours her home would be her own again.

But today, the last of them was still here, lying in bed

in the garden room with a swollen ankle and a constitu-
tion obviously too delicate for the fry-up of leftovers
that Mrs. Benson was stirring in the pan. Mrs. Benson
was a willing cook but a little rough and not always
ready.

"I think I'll give him a grilled sole. With salad and a
few of those boiled potatoes."

"I'll do it, dear," Mrs. Benson offered. "You sit down
and take the weight off your legs."

She was a small, thin woman whose own legs, having
so little weight to carry, were tireless. Every morning
she ran over the whole house with a vacuum cleaner, so
quickly that the dirt was often left a long way behind.

"Shall I set the tray, Mum?" Felicity asked, jumping
up from her chair and setting the table rocking. Her
offer was firmly refused.

She sat down again and glanced at her sister. But Susan, for once, did not volunteer to help. Though she
looked as bright as a poppy in her new red dress, she
was sitting very still, as if trying to escape notice. Felicity sniffed. Hoping Mum won't notice she's been at
Miss Pepper's French scent again, she diagnosed. Afraid
to move in case she wafts it across the kitchen and
drowns out the smell of fried cabbage.

"What are we having for lunch, Mum?" she asked.

Her mother glanced into the frying pan and hesitated.

"Savory cabbage. My own recipe," Mrs. Benson said
proudly. "I used up those cold sausages. And the re-
mains of that bone. It hadn't gone off yet. I had a good
sniff at it. You can't be too careful in this hot weather."

No wonder Dad had gone out. "I'm just going to see Mr. Hillyard," he'd said. "He might be able to suggest something for me. Don't want to lose my contacts." Poor Dad, it wasn't his fault his wine bar had folded, whatever people said. Businesses were going bankrupt all over the place. He wasn't the only one. Nobody could accuse him of not looking for work. He was out almost every day. If his search took him more and more often into the lounge bar of the King's Head, well, many a business deal was settled over a few drinks and a good lunch. She'd heard him say so, and she, at least, believed him. He was always much more cheerful when he came back.

She watched her mother lay the tray for Mr. Ross. An embroidered linen cloth. One of the good glasses—carefully polished, breathed on, and then polished again. A half bottle of white wine—he was in luck! One glass was all she allowed Dad.

"Shall I take it in to him?" Mrs. Benson asked, when everything was ready.

"I can manage, thank you," Mrs. Tait said.

"I'll just come and open the door for you, then."

Like Miss Pepper, Felicity thought, watching the two women leave the kitchen. Miss Pepper had held the door open for Mum and gotten a red rose in return. *Bad luck, Mrs. Benson, you won't get a rose to match your hair. Gray roses don't grow in our garden.*

"Susan," she said.

"Mmm?"

"Why shouldn't you trust charming people?"

"I don't know. I give up. Why shouldn't you?"

"It's not a riddle. I want to know. Why shouldn't you?"

Her sister did not answer. She was smiling to herself —or rather, to an invisible someone close beside her, and fluttering her eyelashes; it was a wonder she could move them at all, they were so heavy with mascara. Now she was pouting and tossing her head, so that her yellow hair swung back from her cheeks. *Very pretty. I wonder who that's in aid of?* Susan was nearly sixteen, just the right age, according to Miss Pepper, to fancy herself in love.

Poor Susan. Watching her sister display her charms to an empty chair, Felicity was glad she was only twelve and too young to be expected to have a boyfriend. Susan was pretty. There was no need for her to worry, but she did. It must be as bad as having to pass an exam.

One I'll never pass, Felicity thought. *I'm too tall. All I see of most boys is the dandruff in their hair.*

Mr. Ross was tall. . . . She had saved his life, and that made a sort of bond between them. "I'll never forget," he'd said, and he'd meant it too. She was sure of that—whatever Miss Pepper had said about not trusting him.

Chapter 7

The sea had retreated, reluctantly at first, each new wave fighting to regain the ground that had been lost. Then, giving up hope, it had swept back over the sands, leaving them to the summer visitors.

Now there were people everywhere, getting in her way. Far too many of them, dotting the water's edge, lying spread out on towels—it was like an obstacle course.

Felicity began to run, jumping over legs and sand castles, being sworn at when her racing feet peppered a picnic with sand. A large shaggy dog, having shaken its wet hair over a dry grandmother, chased after her, barking with excitement.

"Hey! Mind what you're doing!" people shouted, but Felicity was already gone.

She was late. Fifteen minutes late already. If she didn't get there soon, Bony would think she wasn't coming and would go home.

The crowd thinned out as she approached the cliffs.

Even the dog deserted her. The stony beach was unattractive, and the seaweed stank in the sun. There were only two small girls, hunting for crabs in the shallow pools, their heads almost touching. She hurried past, unnoticed, keeping close to the cliff until she was safely out of sight.

The rocks at the foot of the high ledge were uncovered and drying in the sun. She jumped from one to another, feeling the warm stone beneath her bare feet, happy to be alone in her own world, with only the gulls high above her head for company.

And Bony White, of course.

He was already there, kneeling on the flat slab at the bottom of the rockfall, examining its rough surface with frowning concentration.

"What are you looking for?" she asked.

"Blood," he said.

He was a rather heavy boy, with a round chin and dark, curly hair. His father kept a shop in the High Street called the Treasure Chest. Its window was full of brass fenders (dented), silver candlesticks (crooked), china plates and figurines (chipped), and a large tabby cat that was undamaged but not for sale.

Felicity looked over his shoulder.

"Whose blood?" she asked.

"Yours. I suppose you're not wearing that great, dirty snowball on your hand for nothing? Is this the right place? Show me where you were holding on."

It all looked so different with the sea gone. "I dunno. There, I think." She pointed to a wide crack in the rock. They both peered into it intently but could see nothing.

"The sea must've washed it away."

"Pity," he said.

For a boy who didn't like fighting, Bony had surprisingly gruesome tastes. He was nicknamed Bony not because he was thin, but because he collected bones. He had found a sheep's skull on the downs last year, and that had started him off. "Come and see," he'd said when Felicity had wrinkled her nose in disgust. "Bones are beautiful."

They were. The small table in his room bloomed like an ivory garden. The skull, with its long, curving lines, the high arch of a chicken's breastbone, a fish bone like a feather—oddly, they held no suggestion of death. They were too clean, too remote from life. It was only when Bony had said he was hoping to get hold of a cow's skull that she had shuddered.

"You can't hurt animals when they're already dead," he'd protested. "There's no need to look at me like that. I *like* animals. I wouldn't hurt them."

She knew this was true. Bony was a kind boy. But sometimes, seeing him eye her skinny legs wistfully, she couldn't help secretly wondering if he was hoping she'd drop dead so that he could add her to his collection.

"We're supposed to be looking for a suitcase, not blood," she said.

The water had nearly all gone from the gully now, although here and there trapped pools gleamed darkly in the sun. On the far side the line of Gray Gulls marched down into the sea. The one nearest the cliffs was already stranded, sticking up from the smaller rocks like a giant sea-tooth.

She went over and touched it with crossed fingers as she always did, to ward off bad luck. Even in the bright sunlight there was something sinister about the huge rock. Its side was rough and warty and glistened faintly as if with sweat. It crouched on the shore as if waiting for something. She hoped it was not for her.

"Come on!" Bony shouted. "You won't find it over there. Not if the tide was coming in."

"Where will it be, then?" she asked, showing more faith in his charts than he seemed to have himself, for he hesitated, looking sheepish.

"Don't you know?" she asked. "Bony, I thought you knew everything. I thought you'd have worked out the exact spot. All those charts—"

"You wouldn't understand," he said defensively. "It's complicated, see? There's crosscurrents and wind velocity and weight ratio. Things like that. Then it was a spring tide yesterday, remember . . ."

He paused, looking at her hopefully. She knew he wanted her to ask him how you could have a spring tide in August, but she wasn't going to. Once started, Bony could go on for hours, his eyes shining with excitement, telling you things you didn't want to know.

"So it was," she said quickly.

"Most people think spring tides are in spring," he went on, obviously suspecting that she belonged to this ignorant group. She did, but she wasn't going to admit it.

"Silly of them," she said, walking on.

He trotted after her. "They confuse them with the spring equinox—"

"I know."

He looked at her suspiciously and made one last attempt to catch her attention, like someone dangling bright toys in front of a baby.

"It's all to do with the sun and the moon—"

"Oh, shut up!" she said, laughing. "Stop showing off. I know you're clever, Bony. You can tell me about it later. Now we're supposed to be looking for a case."

She had thought it would show up plainly, a bright brown oblong against the greenish, grayish irregular rocks. But as Bony pointed out, it might not be brown or bright any longer, after a night's bashing in the sea.

"It could be half buried under pebbles," he said, "or hidden at the bottom of a pool."

They began searching the gully, peering into dark corners, parting the thick curtains of weed, shifting the debris of the sea with their feet. Wandering about in the hot sunlight, Felicity forgot what she was looking for. She was a magpie collector. Soon her pockets were filled with sea junk: a tiny black stone with a hole in the middle; a piece of sea-frosted glass like a misty emerald; an empty crab shell. She was sitting happily sifting through a drift of small stones, hoping to find jasper or agate, when she heard Bony shouting.

He was standing on some rocks by the cliff, beckoning.

"Have you found it?" she cried, jumping to her feet.

"It's empty!" he called, wanting to save her disappointment.

The suitcase was open, lying facedown at the bottom of a deep pool, its lid hanging on by one hinge. They lifted it out carefully, but there was nothing underneath it, nothing caught in its corners; even the elasticized pocket at the back held only a few scraps of weed and a tiny, translucent shrimp, no bigger than a fingernail.

Felicity jumped into the pool and began searching desperately, digging in the stones and sand in the bottom like a small terrier, careless of her bandaged hand. Bony helped her, moving aside the larger rocks, slipping his fingers into narrow crevices. They found nothing.

"Somebody's been here before us. Somebody's stolen all his things," Felicity said furiously.

But Bony pointed out that the case might have been broken open long before it came to rest in the pool. Its contents could be anywhere, scattered by the racing tide, thrust deep into dark holes, or swept far out to sea.

"I don't suppose we'll ever find them now," he said, looking gloomily around at the landscape of tumbled rocks.

"We must. We must," Felicity insisted, close to tears.

She had not really expected to find the case and had indeed soon stopped looking for it, but somehow that made it all the more bitter, as if Fate were playing a cruel joke on them: You just said you wanted a suitcase. You didn't say it had to be *full*.

They went on looking for another hour. They found scraps of paper, which turned to illegible pulp in their fingers. They found a sodden, stained shoe, too small to belong to Mr. Ross. They found something slimy and horrible that might once have been a sock. The best thing they found was a shirt, possibly once white, it was hard to tell, but it still had a collar and all its buttons. Only one sleeve was torn.

Then the alarm buzzed shrilly on Bony's watch.

"Come on," he said, glancing out to sea. "It's time to go."

"Not yet. We've got another hour. You know it always takes ages on the turn."

"I allowed for that. Low tide was at ten past three. It's five to four now."

"Then we've got another quarter of an hour," she said stubbornly. "You go ahead if you're scared."

He turned away, putting his hands in his pockets and staring out to sea. She felt mean. She had forgotten Bony could not swim. Not that swimming would be much help here, but at least you felt you had a chance. Bony would have none.

"Oh, all right," she said, getting to her feet. Then she stopped. "Just a minute. What's that? There's something there. . . ."

It was the skull of a seabird. She picked it up. Washed clean by the sea and bleached by the sun, it looked like a frozen lily in her brown hand.

"Look what I've found," she said, holding it out.

He took it from her and gazed down at it. She could see he wanted it badly for his collection, but he didn't ask her to give it to him. She remembered all the times he had loaned her money and never nagged at her to pay him back, content to wait until her birthday if necessary.

"You can have it, Bony," she said.

"Are you s-sure?" he stammered, turning pink with pleasure.

She laughed and nodded, and they started walking back over the rocks.

"What do you think it is?" she asked. "A gannet's?"

"It looks too large for that. I'll look it up when I get home. It must've been quite a big bird."

"Perhaps it was an albatross," she suggested. Then she stopped and stared at him. The wind had come up, and it blew coldly through her hair.

"What's the matter?" Bony asked, looking at her curiously. "Is your hand hurting?"

"That's his name!" she said, "Or at least it's what he calls himself. *Albatross*. Albert Ross."

Chapter 8

Felicity was very quiet on the way back. Her hand was hurting again. The filthy, gritty bandage hung down in damp loops, showing the stained dressing underneath. As she followed Bony down the High Street, she began worrying about it.

"You can't go home looking like that or they'll have a fit," Bony had said. "Mum will fix it for you. She's good at wrapping up things."

Perhaps. But china figures and antique jugs were different from hands. Hands had feelings. The dressing had stuck fast to the palm of her hand and was going to hurt when it was pulled off.

She tried to think of something else. That was a mistake. Now she began worrying about Mr. Albert Ross.

All the way back Bony had been telling her how many people had bird names—Swan, Nightingale, Wren, Jay.

"Finch," he said now, waiting for her to catch him up.

The High Street was crowded with summer visitors, clustering round the gift shops, buying postcards and ice cream and calamine lotion for their sunburn. Bony held the bird skull protectively in his hands. It looked very pale against his grubby fingers. As pale as Albert Ross—was that really his name, Felicity wondered, or had he stolen it from the bird? If so, why? The answer came too readily into her mind. "He might be anything," Miss Pepper had said. An impostor? A criminal in hiding?

She frowned, trying to push her unwelcome doubts away.

"What's the matter?" Bony asked, looking at her curiously.

She was tempted to confide in him. But Bony was too sensible. He'd probably think they ought to tell someone. And that someone would tell someone else, and sooner or later it would get back to her mother. Mum wouldn't wait for explanations. She'd turn Mr. Ross out into the street, with his swollen ankle and his shrunk city suit, and nobody in Gull Bay would take him in.

Felicity did not want this to happen. She could be wrong. She usually was. None of the stories she made up about the guests had ever turned out to be true.

"It's only a coincidence," she said firmly.

"What is?"

"His name."

"Of course it is," Bony said, staring at her. "I mean, I haven't met him, but he's not all covered with feathers, is he? Lots of people have funny names. Look at that"— he pointed to the sign above the estate agents—"March and Blunder. Sounds like a military disaster, doesn't it? I can't see why you're making such a fuss—" He broke off, studying her face. "There's something else. You know something I don't," he said accusingly. "What is it?"

"Nothing."

It was no good. His eyes were bright with curiosity. He looked like a dog who had smelled a buried bone and was prepared to dig up the whole garden to get at it.

"You've been peculiar ever since you found this skull," he said. "Why? You must have a reason. . . ." He hesitated, as if remembering how often Felicity had ridiculous ideas, without any help from reason at all. He glanced down at the skull in his hands. "Don't tell me you think he's the ghost of this? You can't be that daft."

A ghost. The spirit of a great bird—now why hadn't she thought of that? It was a far better idea than her own shabby, commonplace suspicions.

"That's clever of you, Bony," she said admiringly.

"You're mad," he told her, shaking his head in disbelief. "Never mind. Here we are. Come in and let Mum fix your bandage."

The Treasure Chest was on the corner, next door to the bookshop. Peering through the window, they could see Mrs. White at the back, talking to a customer.

She was a big, handsome woman, whose clothes were beautiful but always a little odd, as if she'd ransacked a chest in some forgotten attic. Today she was wearing a green silk dress with a dipping hem and had five strings of colored beads round her neck, one of which still had a price tag hanging from it. Her long black hair, held up on the top of her head with colored combs, was beginning to come down.

They could see her mouth opening and shutting, and her plump hands making sweeping gestures that narrowly avoided knocking anything over. Like Watson, her tabby cat, who was also large and light on its feet, she somehow managed to move about the crowded shop without damage.

Seeing them through the window, she waved and beckoned.

"Come on," Bony said, opening the door.

Felicity hung back. "I'm not allowed," she said.

She had broken a china Cupid last year and had been told, kindly but firmly, to come in the side way in future. "You're welcome to play in the back room, love," Mrs. White had said. "Everything's already broken there. You can't do any harm. But come in the side way, not through the shop, eh?"

Today, however, this was forgotten. Mrs. White came forward, holding out her hands.

"Felicity! Come in, come in, dear. We were just talking about you. That was a splendid thing you did. We want to hear all about—" Near enough now to see Felicity clearly, she exclaimed in dismay, "Good heavens, just look at that bandage! What have you been up to? You might have taken better care of her, Sam." This was Bony's real name.

Leaving him mumbling defensively, she swept Felicity off to the kitchen, followed by the other woman, who turned out not to be a customer but only Mrs. Croxley from the bookshop, come in for a gossip.

"Sit down, love," Mrs. White said. "Sam, run to Boots for some bandages. I don't think we've got any. What's that horrible thing you're holding? Take it away."

"It's a bird skull. Felicity gave it to me."

"How kind of her. I hope you thanked her properly. It's lovely," Mrs. White said without blushing. "Run along now."

When Bony had gone, she asked Mrs. Croxley to make them all a cup of tea—"You know where everything is, dear"—and began opening and shutting crowded cupboards and drawers. "Scissors," she muttered, "Antiseptic . . . now where did I put the antiseptic?"

"Will this do?" Mrs. Croxley asked, picking up a bottle from the drain board.

"Well, it's really meant for sinks and toilets. Still, I suppose it might—" She caught sight of Felicity's alarmed face and thought better of it. "Salt!" she cried triumphantly, "Salt water, that's the thing."

"Won't it sting?"

"Probably," Mrs. White admitted. "That's how you know it's doing you good. I'm sure you'll be brave. Don't worry, love. I'm not nearly as inefficient as I look."

She filled a bowl with hot water, added a snowstorm of salt, and sat down beside Felicity.

"Now tell us all about the rescue," she said, but went on talking before Felicity could open her mouth to begin. "Keep your hand still, dear. That's right. I'm just going to snip through this loop. There, that didn't hurt, did it?"

"No."

"I hear the poor young man's been living abroad," Mrs. White went on, snipping through another loop and beginning to unwind the bandage, "In China, wasn't it?"

"Japan," Mrs. Croxley said. "Or was it India? Out east somewhere, anyway."

"They tell me he's a writer," Mrs. White continued. (Who told her? How did they know? How many people had been visiting the garden room while she was in the gully?) "You know, travel books. *Six Weeks in a Tent on the Himalayas*. That sort of thing."

"No wonder he was ill," Mrs. Croxley said, shaking her head. "Not used to roughing it. Comes of a good family, I hear. Rich. Made a lot of money abroad."

"Beautiful manners," Mrs. White agreed. "You can tell at once he's been well brought up."

Felicity stared at them in astonishment. How could they know so much about him? Were they making it all up?

"We'll have to soak this dressing off, love," Mrs. White said. "Dunk your hand in the bowl, there's a good girl."

Bony came in with the new bandage, done up in blue paper. Seeing the pieces of the old one on the table, he began sorting through them for a bloodstained bit for his collection.

"I hear he's lost everything in the sea," Mrs. Croxley was saying. "All his papers and letters of introduction. I don't know how he'll get on. They say he hasn't got a penny."

"He's got twenty-five pounds and eighty-three pence," Felicity said, glad that there was something they didn't already know. "I counted it."

"That won't take him far, dear, will it?" Mrs. Croxley asked with an irritating smile.

"He's not going anywhere. He's staying in bed."

The two women exchanged glances above her head. Bony, having found his piece of bloodstained bandage, put it in his pocket, and, taking a biscuit out of a tin marked "coffee," began to eat it.

"Mrs. Jenkins at the Ship was saying that we ought to make a collection for him," Mrs. Croxley said. "Just to tide him over till he can settle his affairs."

"A collection!" Felicity cried, staring at her. "You mean, you're going to give him *money?*"

They all looked at her in surprise.

"It would only be a loan," Mrs. Croxley said. "We all know how generous your mother is, but we can't expect her to do everything. The rest of us would like a chance to help too." She smiled at Felicity, but her little eyes were sharp. "After all, there's no reason why we shouldn't lend him money, is there?"

"No," Felicity said. But all her doubts came crowding back. Money. Was that what he was after, the stranger who had given himself a bird's name?

"Only you looked so . . . well, almost alarmed at the idea. I wondered if you knew anything—"

"No. No, of course not. It's very kind of you."

"Your mother's not the only one on the charity committee, you know. We all do our bit."

"Yes. I know."

Bony was watching her so intently that she almost felt his glance on her cheek. She turned to look at him. His expression was horribly clever and knowing, as if he could see the unhappy thoughts scuttling round in her head.

If you dare say anything, I'll push your teeth in, she thought, glaring at him.

He did not say anything. Not then.

He saved it until after tea, when they were alone together, sitting on a sagging leather sofa in the big storeroom at the back. Around them, damaged furniture was piled up to the ceiling in high towers that trembled every time a juggernaut went down the High Street. It was like sitting in a cave in an unsteady mountain, both cozy and dangerous.

"You might as well tell me," Bony said. "I've guessed, so there's no point in lying. It was dumb of me not to see it right away. You think that man's given a false name, don't you?"

"No!"

"Yes, you do. You think he's a bad lot. You should have seen your face when they talked about giving him money. But *why*, Fliss? It can't be just because his name sounds like a bird."

She hesitated. "You won't tell anyone?"

"Not unless I have to," he said cautiously.

Not much of a promise. Still, it would have to do. She wanted to tell someone. She wanted someone to laugh at her and assure her it was all nonsense, that her imagination had run away with her. Bony was the best person to do that.

So she told him. "Last night Mum said he seemed to have forgotten his name at first. She said he looked quite blank when they asked him."

"Is that all?" Bony asked incredulously. "He probably hit his head on the rocks in the gully. Got mild concussion. Shook up his brain."

"That's what Miss Tatterson said."

"But you think you know better, of course."

"It was something Mum said. . . . She said when they asked him, he sort of looked vaguely around the room, as if hoping to see his name written up on the walls—"

"And it was?"

"Yes," Felicity said, surprising him out of his mockery. "Right opposite his bed in the garden room. There's a framed chart of seabirds on the wall, with their names printed underneath in big letters: gannet, kittiwake, black-capped gull, and in the middle, where you can't miss it, the largest of them all—"

"An albatross?"

"Not just any albatross. The big one. The wandering albatross."

"The wandering Albert Ross," Bony repeated. "I see."

He was silent, thinking about it. Felicity watched him anxiously.

"It could be just a coincidence, couldn't it?" she asked hopefully. "He could've just forgotten his name for a moment, like you said. Then, seeing the chart, he could've thought, "Albatross! Of course, that's me."

Bony did not answer.

"It could've happened that way, couldn't it?" she insisted. "Like, supposing you'd lost your memory and you caught sight of a bone—"

"I wouldn't sit up in bed and say, 'That reminds me. My name is Bony White,' if that's what you're thinking. For one thing, it isn't. It's Sam White. And for another . . . I dunno . . ." He paused and then said apologetically, "We'll have to tell someone, Fliss. It's probably all nonsense, but we can't risk it. He might be a criminal. He might be . . . anything."

Chapter 9

It was the last thing she'd wanted Bony to say. They had a row about it, sitting at either end of the sagging couch and spitting insults at each other. Felicity called him a pig, a tattletale, a sneak. He told her that she was so stupid, it was a pity that she'd ever learned to talk.

"You pollute the air with your idiot babble," he said grandly.

She wanted to hit him. She wasn't afraid of fighting. With her long arms and hard, knobby fists, she could hold her own with most of the boys in her class. But she knew it was no good hitting Bony. He was a pacifist and didn't seem to care if you called him a coward.

"I have the courage of my convictions," he'd say, and walk away. Or run, if necessary.

She did not want him to go out of the room and straight to his mother, in whom he confided more than she would ever dream of telling hers.

"You promised! You promised you wouldn't tell!" she said unfairly, as he was quick to point out.

"I only said I wouldn't if I didn't have to."

"You don't have to. Nobody's twisting your arm. There's no law says you have to."

"He could be a criminal, Fliss. He could steal all your mum's valuables. Any night."

"He couldn't. He's in the garden room. He can't get into the house after Dad's locked up, so there!"

"He could break a window. He could come creeping up the stairs to your room tonight," he said, trying to frighten her, "How d'you think I'd feel if you got yourself murdered in your bed?"

"*Pleased,*" she said bitterly, and burst into tears.

She did not cry on purpose to get her own way. She might have if she'd thought of it, but it never occurred to her. Crying had never paid off at home when she was small; she no longer regarded it as a possible weapon. She was just tired and on edge, and all her bruises ached.

"Stop it, Fliss," Bony said awkwardly. He did not have any sisters, and tears always moved him. He'd once given away a whole bag of sweets to a small girl sobbing in the playground, even though he was a greedy boy. "You know I wouldn't be pleased."

"It isn't that," she mumbled, wiping her nose on the clean bandage, "It's . . . I thought . . ." She had thought everyone would go on making a fuss of her, as they had last night. She thought a reporter would come round from the *Gullington Echo* to take her picture. She thought somebody'd write to the queen to get her a medal, and everybody would smile at her all day long. But she could not confess these childish desires to Bony.

She was ashamed of them. So she said, "Oh, I dunno. Everybody's gone to the donkey derby except you, and now you're saying he's a murderer."

"I didn't say that, not exactly," Bony said, trying to calm her down. What had happened to her? She was usually a happy-go-lucky sort of girl—once away from her mother, who had a bad effect on her. "I only said he might be one. Anyone might be, come to that. I don't suppose he really is," he added, to cheer her up.

"Then you won't tell about his name?" she asked with such a hopeful look on her thin, smudged face that he agreed weakly. He was too soft; that was his trouble.

"Oh, all right. I won't tell."

She smiled at him, her eyes still shining from her tears.

"Only you be careful, Fliss."

"I will."

"Does your dad lock up properly at night?"

"Every night. And Mum follows him around, checking."

Bony smiled. He did not like Mrs. Tait much, but he trusted her to be efficient. Also, he did not seriously believe that Mr. Ross had given a false name at all. A criminal hiding out, he thought, would come prepared with an alias, not rely on finding a bird chart hanging conveniently on the wall.

Albert Ross . . . albatross, indeed! Farfetched. Just like all Felicity's absurd stories. She was birdbrained, that's all it was. He began making up a rude limerick about her, which he couldn't resist telling her when he'd finished.

"There was a young girl called Felicity,
With a brain of amazing simplicity.
'I'm dim-witted,' she said,
'For it's dark in my head
And I cannot afford electricity.'"

She smiled, but he did not think she appreciated how clever he'd been, so he explained to her that everyone had electrical impulses in their brains—that was what made them work.

"Except you," he said. "You've only got candlepower. Be careful someone doesn't blow it out."

Be careful. Everyone was always telling her to be careful. The gulls, threading their complicated patterns above her head, seemed to repeat the message, "Careful, careful, careful!"

Well, she had told Bony, that was being careful. But then she had persuaded him not to tell anyone else, which she supposed canceled it out. Felicity sighed, uncertain whether to be pleased that she had won her point or not. Perhaps she should tell someone else. Dad?

She thought about it, walking slowly home through the elbowing crowds. Dad would not tell Mum if she asked him not to. He never gave her away, and often, knowing her pocket money was stopped to pay for some breakage, would slip some money into her hand, saying, "Mum's the word," which meant, of course, not a word to Mum.

But would he do anything? Yes, probably. He would go and have a talk with Mr. Ross, man-to-man. She smiled, wondering if he was any better at talking man-to-man than he was at talking man-to-woman. Mum always won their arguments. At home Mum was boss.

What a noise the gulls were making. She looked up at them. Just ordinary, everyday gulls. Not an albatross among them.

Albatross, Felicity thought. There was something about albatrosses. They were supposed to be lucky—or was it unlucky? She frowned, trying to remember.

Pictures flooded her mind, of fire and ice and mist, of a ship on a burning sea and a dead white bird. What on earth—? Then she remembered. She had actually seen them. They were illustrations of a poem Mr. Blakely had read them at school two years ago. *The Rhyme of the Ancient Mariner*, that was it. It was about a sailor who had killed an albatross and brought death and horror down on his ship. The wind had failed, the sea had burned, and terrible monsters had come boiling to the surface like scum. All his friends had died, cursing him for what he had done:

> With his cruel bow he laid full low
> The harmless Albatross.

She smiled as the lines came back to her. It seemed like an omen, a clear warning to take no action against the stranger.

"The harmless Albert Ross," she chanted under her breath, glad of an excuse to do nothing.

Chapter 10

Miss Pepper was sitting in her usual chair on the front veranda, gazing out to sea. The evening sun, streaming through the side window, lit her dyed hair to a blazing red. Even the sky behind her head was tinged with pink, as if the color had run.

"I've been waiting for you," she said when she saw Felicity. "Things have been happening while you were out. I have some good news for you."

"Dad's got a job?"

"No, I'm sorry. Nothing as good as that. Still, I hope you'll be pleased. The *Gullington Echo* rang. They're coming to interview you tomorrow. On Friday your face will be on every breakfast table from here to Deeping Splash. Think of that."

"I wonder how they heard," Felicity said, trying not to look too pleased.

"Somebody told them," Miss Pepper said, adding unexpectedly, "As a matter of fact, it was me. I didn't see why the donkeys should have it all their own way. I'm

afraid they're going to be in the paper too. Dozens of
them. Never mind. I'm sure you'll outshine them all.
Your mother's already let down the hem of your pink
dress—"

"Oh, no! Not that one!"

"I'm afraid so," Miss Pepper said, amused. "Perhaps
you can talk yourself out of it."

Into what? That was the trouble. Felicity glanced
down hopefully at her T-shirt and shorts, but Miss Pepper shook her head.

"No, I don't think your mother would stand for
those, even if they were clean. Her mind seems to be
running toward something grander. Perhaps your sister
can lend you something."

That was an idea. Susan was mean about lending her
things, but then Susan was going out for supper. Her
room would be empty and unprotected. . . .

"Don't you want to hear the rest of the news?" Miss
Pepper went on. "Dr. Feathers called to have a look at
your Mr. Ross. Apparently Miss Tatterson wasn't quite
happy about him."

"What did he say?"

"Oh, that his ankle was coming along nicely, but the
rest of him left a lot to be desired."

"How do you mean?" Felicity asked anxiously.

"I gather that Mr. Ross has only just recovered from
some nasty illness, and being rolled about in the sea
hasn't improved him. Still, Patrick said he can get up
tomorrow, so he can't be so very bad, can he?"

"Patrick?"

"Dr. Feathers. He's an old friend of mine. In fact, he

saw me into the world. You didn't know I was a local
girl, did you? I was born in a house only five miles
away. And now I've come back. I wonder if it was a
mistake." Miss Pepper looked out to sea again. Her face
was in shadow, silhouetted against the deepening gold
of the sky. "I don't know whether it's a good idea to
have too happy a childhood," she said. "It makes the
rest of one's life rather an anticlimax. Perhaps it would
have been better if my parents had beaten me and
locked me in the cellar with all the spiders. Think how
happy I'd have been to get away. Does your mother beat
you?" she asked, turning to Felicity.

"No, she stops my pocket money."

"I'm afraid that doesn't count. Yet you don't always
have the look of a happy child. I wonder. Are you long-
ing to grow up?"

"No."

Miss Pepper looked at her thoughtfully, and Felicity
flushed.

"Are you going back to live in your old home?" she
asked quickly, to distract her.

"No. It's been sold. I've bought a shop in Gullington,
and I'm going to turn it into a classy boutique. You
must come and buy your clothes there when it's ready.
If it ever is ready." She glanced at Felicity and added
slyly, "I'm sorry. I'm not waiting for my drowned lover
to come back to me, merely for the builders to finish my
shop. Very disappointing for you."

Felicity went scarlet and began stammering an inco-
herent apology.

"Oh, I didn't mind," Miss Pepper assured her. "It

was a very romantic story. But I don't think Mrs. Laughton was quite so happy about figuring as a battered wife. Her husband was certainly not pleased. I had quite a job persuading him not to complain to your mother. You know, you really must stop spreading these stories around. Fortunately most of them are too absurd to be believed. But you could get yourself into serious trouble one day. Gossip's quite bad enough when it's true."

She sounded so grave and spoke in a voice so unlike her usual flippant way of talking that Felicity was frightened.

"I didn't spread them around. I only told—" She broke off. Susan. And Bony. And Janine . . .

"One person is one too many," Miss Pepper said. "You ought to know that, living in a small town like this. If you must make up stories, for heaven's sake, change all the names, if you don't want to land up in court on a charge of slander." She smiled and added more lightly, "Don't look so alarmed. I doubt if you'll go to prison this time. Run along now. It must be nearly time for dinner, and you could certainly do with a wash first."

Felicity fled into the house.

The hall was empty. She could hear her mother's voice coming from the kitchen and tried to judge if she was angry. It was hard to tell. Her mother never shouted. But her anger, held in check, was none the less terrible for that. It could simmer on for days.

Had Mr. Laughton complained, in spite of Miss Pepper? She felt it was possible. Probable. He was a stout, red-faced man who did not look as if he had a sense of humor.

Felicity felt like a criminal. She had ruined her family. Mum would never forgive her. Never. She was always saying the Fairweather depended on personal recommendation, and who would tell their friends to come here now? Nobody. She had told so many stories, most of them scandalous.

Next summer, all the rooms would be empty. There would be no money coming in, except for Dad's unemployment check, and that wouldn't pay for a new roof. The house would crumble about their heads, and it would be all her fault. . . .

The sensible part of her mind, revolted by such gloomy fancies, told her not to be so silly. It wouldn't come to that. It would all blow over. Things always had before.

But she was too nervous to listen to it. Hearing footsteps on the stairs, she was immediately convinced it was Mr. Laughton coming to confront her, and she bolted into the garden.

On the far side of the lawn, the two small girls from Room 4 were playing with a red ball and did not notice her. She stood watching them for a minute, feeling the fresh air cooling her cheeks. Then she looked toward the garden room. The light was already on, though the curtains were not yet drawn. She walked quietly across the grass and looked through the window.

Mr. Ross was sitting up in bed, reading a newspaper. As she watched, he put it down on his knees and sighed. His thin fingers began beating a nervous tattoo on his bedside table. Suddenly he looked toward the window and caught sight of her before she had time to duck. His face lit up with a delighted smile, and he beckoned.

"Oh, I am pleased to see you," he said when she came into the room. "I've been so worried. That horrible, dangerous place—I never should have let you go there. I've been imagining dreadful things. . . ."

As he spoke, he glanced quickly at her empty hands.

"I went to tea with Bony, that's why I'm back late," she explained, "We found your case in the gully, but I'm afraid it must've busted open and your things been washed out to sea. We looked everywhere, but—"

"Never mind," he said quickly. "You're safe back, and that's all that matters." Indeed, he did not look disappointed. There was only relief on his face. "Come and talk to me." He gestured at the chair by the bed.

"I can only stay a minute. I ought to be getting ready for supper."

But she sat down. It was comforting to be with someone so obviously pleased to see her. And it was cozy in the garden room with the light on and the summer day fading outside. She felt calmer. Things were not so bad, after all.

Looking into his smiling face, she could not understand how she had ever suspected Mr. Ross of anything. He looked so friendly and so innocent. Even when he began coughing, the dry, rapid, articulated cough, she no longer doubted that it was real. Dr. Feathers had seen him and left him some medicine. She could see the bottle on his bedside table, and a small white box that must contain pills. He was a genuine invalid.

"We left your case in the gully," she told him when he'd finished coughing. "Bony said it was too far gone to be repaired. But we found this . . ."

She put her hand down the neck of her T-shirt, where she often kept things that were too big to go in the pockets of her shorts. "It's only one of your shirts," she said, in case he was hoping for something more important.

She brought it out. It was still slightly damp and reeked of the sea. It was also far more tattered and stained than she'd remembered. It looked like a rather horrible rag.

"Thank you," he said, taking it from her. His mouth twitched.

"It's still got all its buttons."

"I shall treasure them."

Their eyes met, and they began to laugh.

"I'll throw it in the dustbin," Felicity said, holding out her hand, but he shook his head and told her he wanted to keep it as a souvenir.

"I've got something for you too," he said, and, picking up the small white box, gave it to her. "I asked Miss Tatterson to get it for me. I told her just what I wanted for you. I hope you like it."

Inside the box, lying on a nest of cotton wool, was a small silver brooch of a gull flying.

"It's beautiful!" she cried, her eyes shining with delight.

"I hope it brings you luck whenever you wear it. I wish it could be more, but . . ." He shrugged.

"It's the best present I've ever had," she told him.

It was true. She'd rather have it than a bucketful of roses. He had told Miss Tatterson exactly what to get. He had chosen it especially for her.

The hall was full of guests moving toward the dining room, for the gong had just gone off. She waited politely to let them by, saying good evening and agreeing that it had been a lovely day. She had quite forgotten her previous worry.

Then she felt a hand on her shoulder. Looking up, she saw Mr. Laughton—and remembered.

"I want a word with you, young lady," he said, drawing her aside.

"Oh."

"You might well say 'oh.' Guilty conscience, eh? You listen to me, my girl. I don't like being accused of beating my wife. It's a damned lie, and I could have you for slander. She fell down them front steps, as half the people here can tell you, having seen it happen with their own eyes."

"I'm sorry."

"So you should be. If you were my child, I'd take a strap to you. I'm warning you. You're to stop telling your stories or I'll go straight to your dad. D'you understand?"

"Yes."

"I want your word on it."

"I promise."

"No more stories?"

"No more stories," she agreed, looking uneasily toward the open dining room door and wondering where her mother was. He had such a loud voice.

"All right. I'll let you off this time," he said, and, looking down at her nervous face, added more kindly, "Cheer up. I'm not going to eat you."

"Thank you," she said, smiling weakly. Her hand went up to touch the brooch.

"That's pretty," he said. "A sea gull, isn't it?"

"It's a lucky albatross," she told him. "Nothing can harm you when you wear it."

"So that's why I let you off," he said, laughing. "And I thought it was my soft heart."

Chapter 11

The front door of the Fairweather was open. A few summer kids, scattered over the hall and stairs, were squabbling like gulls. As Bony waited for an old gentleman to totter past, he heard Felicity's name.

"No, not the fair one. The dark one. Felicity," a child said.

"What's happened?" he asked anxiously.

"Happened?" a boy said blankly. "Nothing. Why?"

"I thought one of you said something about Felicity."

"Oh, that. She's going to be in the paper. Only the local rag," the boy said, sounding superior.

"Big deal," Bony said, and went through into the back garden.

There were several people on the lawn. He saw Felicity. She was all tarted up. Her long hair, usually as shaggy as a dog's, was flat and shiny, her denims unnaturally clean, and she was wearing a bright red shirt with big blue dots. Very fancy.

She hadn't seen him because she was busy fending off

her sister, who looked as mad as fire. Bony moved closer.

"It's mine!" he heard Susan say in a shrill hiss. "New. I haven't even worn it yet. Go and take it off—"

"But I've nothing."

"I don't care! Give it back!"

Good Lord! She's going to strip it off her. No. Ma Tait's going over to break it up. Pity.

Bony turned his attention to the man sitting in the deck chair, his bandaged foot on a low stool.

So that was Mr. Albert Ross.

A weed. Thin and pale. A sick face. Untidy blond hair. Age? Difficult to tell. Youngish.

Harmless enough, Bony thought, and was conscious of a feeling of relief, as if some small, foolish part of him had been worried about Felicity all the time.

The man was talking to a smiling old lady, who was showing him some sort of knitted shawl or blanket. Bony edged nearer to hear what they were saying.

". . . really beautiful," Mr. Ross said. His voice was weak and a little husky, as if he had not so much a frog, but a tadpole, in his throat. "Did you really make it yourself? How clever you are. That deep red against the lilac—exquisite."

Smarmy. Too smooth by half. What's he after? Bony wondered. Perhaps the old girl's rich. No. Wouldn't be staying here if she was.

The old lady went back into the house, leaving the knitted shawl over Mr. Ross's legs. The smart, red-headed woman had joined the group round Felicity.

What was her name? Salt? No, Miss Pepper. Felicity said she dyed her hair. Probably true.

Bony was not offended that no one was paying any attention to him. He was honest enough to admit that he probably wasn't very visible, since he was standing extremely close to a large shrub. So close, in fact, that every time he breathed, the leaves shook. He was content to watch and listen. Felicity often accused him of having no imagination, but she was wrong. It was just that Bony preferred to have a foundation of facts before he started building castles in the air. He had come here to be an observer—

It was a shock to realize, when he glanced back at the man in the deck chair, that he, himself, was being observed.

The man's round, bright eyes were staring at Bony. He looked a little amused. He beckoned. Reluctantly Bony left his concealment of leaves and walked over to him.

"Hullo," Mr. Ross said. "I haven't seen you before, have I? Are you staying here?"

"No. I'm a friend of Felicity's. Sam White."

"Sam White," the man repeated. "Then, Bony White must be your brother?"

"No. That's me too."

"So you're Bony!" Mr. Ross exclaimed, sounding as delighted as if he'd been waiting all his life for this meeting, "Felicity's told me all about you."

"She doesn't know all about me," Bony said, revolted. "She probably made most of it up. She always does."

The man smiled. Bony was a fair-minded boy, and he

had to admit that it was a nice smile. Friendly. Like he was inviting you to share a joke at his own expense. "Silly thing to say," Mr. Ross admitted. "I only meant she told me you helped her look for my case. It was very kind of you. And brave too. I wouldn't go near that dreadful place again for the world."

Soft soap. *Trying it on* me *now*, Bony thought. *Wants everyone to like him. Well, count me out.*

"It's all right if you know what you're doing," he said curtly.

"And I'm sure you always do." The man had sensed Bony's unfriendliness. His smile faded. Suddenly he looked very tired and ill and sad.

Bony felt sorry for him. He couldn't help it.

"Well, I ought to know. I was born here," he said quickly. "Dad taught me all about tides and currents when I was small. It's stupid to take risks. Dad says only fools get themselves cut off by the tide—" He broke off, flushing, realizing he was only making matters worse.

"It was silly of me," Mr. Ross agreed, looking ashamed.

"It wasn't your fault," Bony said kindly. "It's the council's. They should put up better signs. It's very dangerous out by the Gulls."

He began to explain about the tides and the crosscurrents and the pull of the sun and the moon. Mr. Ross listened to him with more respect than anyone had ever shown before. Even the teachers at school often said, "Yes, yes, Bony. That's enough. Give someone else a chance to show off." He was not used to such interest, and it went to his head. He found himself telling Mr. Ross all about his collection of bones.

"How fascinating," Mr. Ross said, impressed. "What a lot you know."

It was nice to talk to an intelligent person for a change. Bony, carried away with enthusiasm, did not notice the men from the *Echo* arrive.

Mr. Ross did. His eyes, looking past Bony, opened very wide, and he said, sounding almost alarmed, "Oh, no! Is that the press? I thought they weren't coming till this afternoon."

Bony looked round and saw Mrs. Tait and Felicity crossing the grass, followed by two young men, one with a camera over his shoulder. Mr. Ross began struggling to get out of his deck chair.

"Think I'll go to my room," he said with a nervous smile. "Don't want to get in the way."

He was too late.

"Ah, Mr. Ross, please don't get up," Mrs. Tait said, brushing past Bony. "These gentlemen would like a picture of you and Felicity together. But I'm sure they won't mind if you sit down."

"Oh, no! No, please!" Mr. Ross seemed to be in a positive panic of modesty. "I'd only spoil it. I take a terrible photograph. Honestly. Much better just to have a pretty girl against a background of roses."

Felicity? Pretty? Bony looked at her. Her face was flushed and smiling. Seeing him, she winked and wriggled her shoulders, as if to say, "Silly fuss, isn't it?" But she was obviously enjoying herself immensely. Her fingers kept touching a small silver brooch pinned to the scarlet blouse: a gull flying. Bony's mind made a leap without the help of a single hard fact. Mr. Ross had given it to her. She's got a crush on him.

He stepped back, and it was as if a spell had broken. He saw Mr. Ross, smiling and protesting, coughing and apologizing. "I'm sorry. I'm holding you up. Please leave me out." How he smiled and smiled, sugar-sweet, so charming, so modest. . . .

Bony wanted to vomit.

How could he have fallen for it? He had no excuse. He'd heard Mr. Ross buttering up the old lady: "Did you really make it yourself? How clever you are." And not five minutes later he was lapping up the same sickly goo. "How fascinating. How much you know."

Oh, Lord, Bony thought with disgust. *And I fell for it!*

He could have kicked himself, remembering his pride and pleasure, how he'd felt that he'd found someone at last who shared his own interests. A friend! That hollow, simpering smirk of a man. Bony had seen snakes he would have trusted more.

"You look thoughtful," a voice said, startling him. He turned his head and saw Miss Pepper. She was not speaking to him but to a sallow gray-haired woman he hadn't seen before. "What do you think of our young man of the sea?" she went on. "Delightful, isn't he?"

Though she spoke lightly, her words seemed to trail shadows, distorting their meaning. The other woman seemed to understand her, however, because she laughed.

"I wish you wouldn't call him that," she said. "It's my

fault he's still here. Perhaps I should have let them pack him off to hospital that first night."

"They won't find him easy to shift now," Miss Pepper said. "He's too comfortable. I've met his type before. Born sponger. Let him get his foot in the door and the next thing you know, he's one of the family."

"Oh, come, it's only two days," the other woman said, as if trying to be fair. "And he's not well."

"As he keeps reminding us. That stupid little cough. I could do better myself. He's a phony. Look at him now. What a fuss he's making. He really doesn't seem to want his photograph taken, does he? I wonder why."

"Vanity," the other woman suggested. "He can hardly be looking his best at the moment."

"Perhaps," Miss Pepper said.

Bony longed to ask her what she was thinking, but the women did not know he was there and might be cross with him for listening to their conversation. He had turned away, thinking he might as well go home, when he heard Miss Pepper say, "Young Felicity seems to be getting moony over him. Silly girl. I hope she doesn't get hurt. I'm becoming quite attached to her. I can't think why."

"Probably because she's the first child you've ever spoken to," the other woman said. "Don't worry. A spot of hero worship never hurt anyone. She'll grow out of it."

Hero worship! That drip—a hero?

I hate him, Bony thought. *I'll never let him make a mug of me again. Never. And I'll put Felicity against him too. I'll tell her what a sham he is. No, that's no good. She'd refuse to believe me.*

He thought about it, walking home through the hot streets, listening to the gulls screaming curses over his head. *I'll find out all about him*, he decided. *I'll prove he's a liar. See if I don't.*

The photographs in the *Gullington Echo* were disappointing. Felicity had come out rather well, but Mr. Ross seemed to have sunk into his borrowed dressing gown. He must have moved at the last minute too. Half hidden by the dark collar, his face was a pale blur.

"It's not very good of him, is it?" Felicity asked, showing the photograph to Bony.

"Unrecognizable," he said.

Chapter 12

It was as if Mr. Ross had cast a spell over the Fair-weather Guest House. The building itself seemed to shimmer in a luminous haze. As for the people inside, they were all charmed by him—such a nice young man, so polite, so interested in everybody, they said, and so modest, he never wanted to talk about himself. He had even brought the good weather with him, for the days since he'd come were hot and bright, with a warm wind blowing off the sea.

Even Miss Pepper had been won over. The builders had nearly finished her shop, and now that the painters were about to start, she suddenly got into a panic, changed her mind a hundred times. For a whole day she sat on the veranda, with color charts spread all over the little table in front of her, running her fingers through her hair till it looked like a forest fire. Everyone offered advice. It was Mr. Ross's she took.

"He's really got a marvelous color sense," she told Felicity. "Original. If my shop does well, I've a good mind to offer to take him on as a partner."

Felicity hated the idea, but she didn't say so. She didn't want Mr. Ross to work with Miss Pepper in Gullington. She wanted him to stay at the Fairweather forever. Mum liked him. Everybody liked him.

Except Bony White.

Bony White had turned against him. He told Felicity that she had been right, after all. Mr. Ross had given a false name. Must have. He was false right through, from the top of his fluffy yellow hair to the bottom of his limping feet. To anyone with a discerning nose, he stank of fishiness.

"Don't be silly," Felicity said. "Mum told Dad to have a talk with him, and Dad says he's all right."

"Your father's a . . . a nice man," Bony said. "Too honest to see through people."

"You mean he's gullible."

"Gullible," Bony said, staring at the silver brooch she wore all the time now. "You said it. Gullible."

"Oh, go away, Bony."

But Bony seemed unable to stay away. He hated Mr. Ross, but he hung round him, like a small terrier waiting for a chance to attack. One morning, when Felicity and Mr. Ross were in the garden together, Mr. Ross in his deck chair and Felicity sitting on the grass at his feet, they saw Bony stomping over the lawn toward them.

He looked tired, as if he'd been sitting up half the night, but there was an air of determination about him. He was up to something.

"Good morning, Bony," Mr. Ross said politely. He was always polite to Bony, though he must have guessed the boy did not like him. "Come and join us. We were talking about fossils. Felicity tells me there's a quarry near here that's still worked by hand."

"Yes," Bony said, but he refused to be interested in fossils today. He sat down on the grass beside Felicity and began asking Mr. Ross questions about China.

It was soon obvious to the three of them that he knew far more about China than Mr. Ross did.

He's been cramming, Felicity thought. That's why he looks bug-eyed. He's read every book on China he could lay his grubby hands on. He's trying to trap him.

Half angry, half amused, she listened in silence, feeling more like a tennis umpire than a judge, her head turning from one to the other as they talked. She began awarding them points in her mind.

Bony—eight for effort. Five to Mr. Ross for a well-timed fit of coughing. Bony—seven for refusing to be distracted. Mr. Ross—six for a neat evasion. Bony was winning, she thought, biting her lip.

"I'm sorry, Bony," Mr. Ross said at last, smiling and lifting his hands as if to acknowledge defeat. "I'm afraid I don't really know very much about China. I was only in Hong Kong for a little while, and that was some time ago now. Big cities are all alike, aren't they? I did go to the mainland once. We were taken round a factory, but I can't even remember what it was making. Big rooms full of noisy machines. I'm afraid I found it very boring."

Ten out of ten, Felicity thought gleefully. She felt almost sorry for Bony. He was red in the face and looked absolutely dumbfounded.

"But I thought you'd been exploring bamboo for-ests," he said. "I thought you'd written a book about pandas."

"Pandas? Good heavens, no," Mr. Ross said, looking surprised. "Whatever gave you that idea?"

Felicity giggled. But when Bony looked at her with furious reproach, guessing too late where that story had come from, she felt guilty and decided to help him. Be-sides, she wanted to know too.

"Which country were you in?" she asked.

"Oh, I was wandering all over the place," he said. "I'm a very restless person. I like to keep on the move."

Six out of ten, she thought, but she felt disappointed. He might have told her. Almost as if guessing her feel-ings, he added, "I think I liked India best."

"India," Bony repeated, with so much triumph in his voice that he might just as well have shouted aloud, "Got you!"

Making some excuse—something about helping his father to load up their van—he left them.

Felicity looked after him thoughtfully. She was not stupid. She knew exactly what he was going to do. As soon as he was out of sight, he'd start running. He'd run back to the library with all his books on China and change them for books on India. Poor Bony, another night's studying. Then he'd be back tomorrow to try again. Bony hated to be beaten. He was always cross when Felicity got better marks at school than he did. He liked to pretend she was stupid. In fact, he really pre-ferred all his friends to be a little dim so that he could instruct them.

Bad luck, Bony, she thought. *I'm just as clever as you are. Go on, run as fast as you can. Take every book on India out of the library. I don't care. There's a bigger library in Gullington, and that's where I'm going this afternoon. See you tomorrow, mate.*

Mr. Ross was sitting on the front veranda talking to two of the guests when Felicity got back from Gullington. She hung round until they had gone, and then took their place.

"Hullo," Mr. Ross said, smiling at her. "Did you have a nice afternoon?"

"I went to the library in Gullington."

"Are you fond of reading?" It was an idle question. He was not looking at her but at a small brown pebble he was rolling between his fingers.

"I got some books on India," she said, taking them out of her bag and putting them on the table between them.

"Oh?" He glanced at her quickly and then down at the books. "Are you interested in India?" he asked after a short pause.

She did not answer.

"It's a fascinating country," he said, watching her. "You must go there one day. I'm sure you'd love it."

"Yes." She opened one of the books and flicked through the pages. "The photographs are nice," she said. "There's the Taj Mahal. They say it's very pretty by moonlight."

"Yes, it is," he agreed smoothly. He looked amused.

"I thought you might like to borrow them," she said,

pushing the books toward him. "I mean, it's nice to see photographs of places you've been to, isn't it?"

"Yes," he said, adding slyly, "It helps refresh one's memory, doesn't it? In case one's forgotten."

Their eyes met, and they smiled at each other. It was a conspirator's smile. Poor Bony, he didn't stand a chance against them.

But when Mr. Ross had gone back into the house, taking the books with him, Felicity felt suddenly confused.

What am I doing? she wondered. *What game am I playing? I gave him those books because . . . because I don't believe he's ever been to India. But that means—*

She shook her head, not wanting to complete the sentence in her mind, but it was no good—*that means I think he's a liar.*

Her fingers went up to touch the silver brooch.

I don't care, she thought stubbornly, *I like him. I'm on his side. Lots of people tell lies. I do myself. I'm always making up stories. It's no worse than that. And I know he's good. He must be.*

She heard the sea sighing in the bay, being pulled backward and forward by the sun and the moon. She wondered if it felt as confused as she did.

Bony, holding the bird's skull in his hands, had asked scornfully, "Don't tell me you think he's the ghost of this? You can't be that daft."

Could she? Did she really believe Mr. Ross was the spirit of a bird? No. Perhaps not. Perhaps it was too difficult, even for her.

And yet, when she remembered the stranger appearing suddenly out of the falling spray, his eyes as bright as a bird's, his pale hair feathering in the wind, then it was easy to believe. When she sat at his feet listening to his airy tales of distant journeys—yes, then she believed he was what he called himself: albatross, the wanderer.

Chapter 13

Bony turned up again the next morning. His head was aching fit to burst, his eyes were itching from lack of sleep, but he walked in jauntily, beaming. He was looking forward enormously to exposing Mr. Ross. It never occurred to him that he might find his enemy prepared.

Mr. Ross was more than willing to talk about India. In fact, Bony thought he would never stop talking about India. Though his voice was still weak and husky and punctuated by fits of coughing, he made no attempt to change the subject.

He spoke about temples gleaming in the sunlight—and gave their names, the districts in which they could be found, the religions they practiced. He described women, bright as hummingbirds in their saris, washing clothes in the slow, wide, brown river—and he knew the river's name, where it had come from, and where it was going, the types of boats that rode upon its back and the cargoes they carried.

His voice became fainter and fainter, but he kept on

telling Bony about India. And Felicity sat at his feet, gazing up at him with a silly smile on her face.

Bony was silent now, his face red with humiliation. Having crammed the whole of India and China into his head in the last two nights, he got them muddled up. He said Peking when he meant Bombay, and Mr. Ross gently put him right. He became afraid to ask another question in case he made a fool of himself. As soon as he could, he made an excuse to leave.

"I'm sorry, Bony," Mr. Ross said apologetically. "I'm afraid I've been talking too much. But it was so nice to have an intelligent listener."

"Bony's ever so clever," Felicity joined in eagerly. "He always comes in top at school."

Ugh! Bony thought with disgust.

He did not even look at Felicity, not wanting to see the triumph on her face. She needn't think he was going to give up.

Sooner or later, Mr. Albert Ross, he thought, *sooner or later I'm going to get you.*

When Bony had gone, Felicity glanced up at Mr. Ross, rather like a puppy hoping for a reward after a difficult trick. She had not enjoyed Bony's defeat as much as she'd expected to, and hoped Mr. Ross would say something to make her feel better. She wanted him to smile at her gratefully and tell her that she'd saved him once again.

But he only said, "I hope I didn't bore your friend. I'm afraid when I start talking about India, I'm apt to go on and on. It's such a fascinating country."

She stared at him. His eyes met hers innocently, without the suspicion of a wink. He spoke as if she'd never given him the books the previous night. She began to wonder if she'd imagined the whole thing.

"He's a nice boy, isn't he?" Mr. Ross went on. "I hope I didn't drive him away with my lecture. I thought he left rather abruptly."

"Oh, he'll be back," Felicity said carelessly.

She was wrong. Bony did not come back. Days passed, and he did not come near the Fairweather. Sometimes she saw him in the town with a group of boys, all too busy talking to notice her. More often he was by himself, scuttling quickly in the opposite direction, as if he'd seen her first and was avoiding her. Whenever she went round to the Treasure Chest, he was out. Or so his mother told her.

Still sulking, Felicity thought, shrugging her shoulders, *See if I care.*

She did. To her surprise she missed him very much. Her best friends, Sally and Rachel, lived miles away, right on the other side of Gullington. Besides, they were always doing things she couldn't afford, like riding ponies or windsurfing. Even the bus fare was often beyond her.

It was useful to have a local friend, only five minutes' walk away. She had known Bony all her life, and though she often made fun of him, she secretly preferred his company to anyone else's. He was always willing to go to the gully or up on the downs to look for fossils and bones. He helped her with her homework, shared his sweets with her, and occasionally loaned her money. In return she listened to his silly limericks and let him lecture her on everything under the sun. She didn't really mind. He couldn't help it. He pushed so much into his head, it was bound to come out of his mouth. Besides, sometimes it was quite interesting.

She began to worry in case she had lost his friendship forever. It was the fault of that stupid record Susan kept playing over and over again in her room:

> This is the end.
> This is the final day.
> You've gone too far, my friend.
> This is the parting way,
> This is the end.

The monotonous, doleful tune, throbbing into her attic room, got on Felicity's nerves, and she hammered on the wall.

Susan shouted back at her, her voice thickened with tears. She was always shutting herself in her room and crying nowadays. It was no good trying to be sympathetic. You could hardly talk to her without getting your head snapped off.

"Go away! Get out! Leave me alone, can't you?"

"Don't tease her, Felicity," their mother had said. "Can't you see she's upset?"

"Of course I can. I'm not blind. I was only trying to cheer her up."

"Well, don't. Just leave her alone."

"What's the matter with her?"

"Oh, boyfriend trouble, I expect," Mrs. Tait had said with an indulgent smile. "She's at a difficult age."

As far as Felicity was concerned, Susan had been at a difficult age for years, but Mum had always favored her. They would sit in corners having womanly conversations and stop talking when Felicity came into the room.

Felicity sighed and trailed downstairs. She was lonely. Susan was a dead loss. Dad was always out looking for work. All the old guests had gone, except for Miss Pepper, who now spent all day in Gullington. Most of the new lot were only staying a week. It seemed hardly worth remembering their names.

Worst of all, she saw less of Mr. Ross. Now that his ankle was better, he did not seem to belong to her anymore. Now he was everybody's friend. He had breakfast with the other guests. He talked as much to them and to Susan and Mum as he did to her. Recently he had started going out for the whole day, taking sandwiches with him for lunch, and she would not see him till evening. She wanted to go with him, but now that her hand had healed, she had to help with the chores in the morning. However much she hurried, he was already gone by the time she finished.

Going into the kitchen now, she asked her mother if she could do her share of the work before breakfast.

"You can't make the beds when the guests are still in them, silly," Mrs. Tait said.

"I could swop with Susan. I could lay the tables—"

"Oh, no. I'm not letting you loose on our crockery. I've lost enough china that way, thank you."

Felicity turned away. It was useless talking to her mother. It always was. Her mother called her back.

"Felicity?"

"Yes?"

"Sit down, dear. I want to talk to you." But when Felicity sat down obediently by the table, her mother seemed to forget her and went on washing up in silence.

It was hot in the kitchen. A fly buzzed at the window. Above their heads, the vacuum cleaner hummed. Felicity fidgeted, wondering uneasily what her mother wanted. She made a tower of sugar lumps while she waited. It fell over. She bent down to retrieve a piece from the floor, hit her head on the table coming up, and set everything rattling.

"For heaven's sake, child," her mother said, turning round irritably, "leave things alone. I've never known anyone like you—can't you sit still for a minute? Put your hands in your lap. And don't kick the table. Don't *move!*"

"I don't know what I'm waiting for," Felicity grumbled.

"I want to talk to you about Mr. Ross."

"Oh."

Her mother came and sat down beside her, pulling off her rubber gloves. "Now I know you're fond of him, dear," she said. "Of course you are. You saved his life. We all feel warmly toward people we've helped. It's only natural. But we mustn't let ourselves get carried away, must we?"

"What are you talking about?" It sounded rude. It

always surprised Felicity how often her simple questions irritated people.

"I don't want you hanging around Mr. Ross all the
time," Mrs. Tait said sharply. "It's not suitable. You're
only a child. And you're not to go out with him on his
walks, do you understand? I mean it, Felicity."

Felicity stared at her in astonishment. Mum was always talking and laughing with Mr. Ross. She made
him sandwiches to take out for his lunch, which was
more than she did for the other guests. She invited him
into their private sitting room in the evenings. She'd
even started playing again on the old battered upright
that she hadn't touched for years. Mr. Ross had said
anyone could tell she had talent, and what a pity it was
that she had let the piano get out of tune.

"I thought you liked him," Felicity said.

"Yes. Yes, I do," her mother agreed. "I'm not saying
anything against him. But, after all, he is a stranger—"

"A stranger! Why, you were only saying last night
that he seemed quite one of the family."

Her mother did not look pleased to be reminded of
this. "Oh, well, one says things like that. But when it
comes to the point, we really know nothing about him."

"We do! He's told us—"

"He's told us a great many fascinating stories about
India. He's told us his trunks are being sent on by rail
and sea and will take weeks to arrive. He's told us he's
rung up his agent over there to have his money trans-
ferred. . . . Oh, it's all perfectly reasonable, no doubt,
but I'll feel happier when something actually arrives.
As Mrs. Benson was saying—"

"She doesn't know. Dad had a talk with him. Dad was satisfied."

"Yes," her mother agreed. "Your father was satisfied." The tone of her voice put Dad in his place. A man too easily taken in. A man who had thrown up a good job to start a wine bar, become his own best customer, and gone bust in the shortest possible time. Everyone had seen it coming. Everyone sympathized with her mother. Felicity was the only exception, and she was on Dad's side because she loved him, not because she could think of anything to say in his defense. So she kept silent.

Her mother sighed and said, "I think I'd better have a word with Mr. Ross myself."

Considering she talked to him every day, this might have sounded odd, but Felicity knew what she meant. She was going to cross-examine Mr. Ross, turn him inside out, pin him down to hard facts, like a moth. And this time there were no books Felicity could give him to protect himself with.

"You won't ask him to leave, will you?" Felicity asked anxiously. "You couldn't be so mean. He's got nowhere to go. And he's so happy here. He's always saying so. Please, Mum, don't turn him out!"

"We'll have to see," was all her mother would say. She got up and went to the sink. There was only the sound of soapy water swishing and the tiny clinking of china. Her back looked stiff and unbending.

"He was only saying yesterday how kind you are," Felicity said. "He said you were a wonderful person and I was lucky to have a mother like you. Everyone's always telling me how generous you are. And it's true, Mum. You are kind."

Her mother turned to look at her. She did not appear as pleased as Felicity had hoped.

"I'm overwhelmed," she said dryly. "But don't overdo it, Felicity, will you? I'm not used to flattery from you, and I'm not sure I like it. I'm beginning to think Mr. Ross is having a bad effect on you."

"You're cross if I'm rude, and now you're cross when I try to be polite," Felicity shouted angrily. "Why don't you make up your mind what you want? You're so stupid!"

She slammed out of the house. A gentle wind was blowing off the sea, and it cooled her hot cheeks. From the open attic window the sound of her sister's record drifted down to her:

> This is the end.
> This is the final day.
> You've gone too far, my friend . . .

Oh, Lord, she shouldn't have had a row with Mum. Now Mum would be in a bad temper that would last all day and spill out on everyone within her reach.

She'll turn out Mr. Ross just to spite me, Felicity thought unhappily. *I know she will. I must find him. I must warn him to keep out of her way till it's had time to blow over. I must find him. . . .*

Chapter 14

The seafront was crowded. Everywhere she looked, she saw faces, pink and red and brown, like colored balloons floating past her eyes. None of them was his. With his pale hair and skin, he should stand out like snow in summer, but like snow in summer, he had melted away.

She looked at the bus stop, wondering if he had gone into Gullington to help Miss Pepper dress her window for next week's gala opening. Was it likely? Yes, she decided gloomily.

"Are you in the queue, dear?" a woman asked her.

"No," she said, turning away. She had no money to follow them by bus.

She cut through to the High Street and peered, without much hope, into café and shop windows, but he was not there. Two girls from her school, with rolled towels under their arms, asked her to come swimming, but she shook her head.

"I can't. I'm looking for someone."

She heard them giggling together as they walked on,

and Felicity flushed, convinced they were laughing at her. Had the whole of Gull Bay been watching her as she'd wandered about looking for Bony? Perhaps they'd thought she'd been trailing foolishly after Mr. Ross. . . .

She began to walk quickly, her head up, trying to look like someone going somewhere with a purpose. She turned briskly into a side road—and stopped.

Some way down on the left, Bony was standing in a doorway, hiding. His back was flattened against the green paint of the door. As she watched, he peered furtively round one of the pillars, then ducked back. She looked past him, expecting to see a gang of toughs out for trouble, but saw only one thin figure in the distance, limping out of sight. Mr. Ross.

She began to run. Bony had emerged from his doorway and was hurrying after Mr. Ross, but her legs were longer than his. She pounced on him before he had gone more than a few yards.

He squealed, and then, seeing who it was, said reproachfully, "You shouldn't do that. You could give someone a heart attack that way."

"Serve you right if I had. What d'you think you're doing?"

"Nothing."

"You were spying on Mr. Ross. Following him."

He shrugged. "Just playing detectives."

"Detectives!" she said scornfully, as if she'd never played Sherlock Holmes to Bony's Dr. Watson all summer before.

"And now you've made me lose him," he complained.

She looked down the empty street and began to run again. But she had wasted too much time. When she reached the concrete blister of the traffic circle, there was no one in sight. Three narrow roads wound away in different directions: to the sea, to the cliffs, to the downs. Had he walked very quickly round one of the concealing bends? Or gone into one of the houses? Or vanished into thin air?

"Do you want to know where he usually goes?" Bony asked, coming up beside her.

She hesitated, then nodded sulkily.

"Follow me," he said.

He took the road to the cliffs. Felicity followed, puzzled. It was the last way she would have expected. The road was very steep, and it seemed an odd choice for a man with a weak ankle. Felicity began to wonder if Bony was deliberately misleading her, but she did not say anything, curious to see where he would take her.

The road ended in a parking space overlooking the bay. Now they were on the cliff path. It was very hot. On one side there were low gorse bushes, their gold flowers already tarnished, their scent heavy and thick. On the other, a wire fence, a few yards of turf, and then nothing but sea and air. There were no people in sight.

They went up and up. The wind was stronger here, a cool wind blowing in from the sea. At last Bony stopped. Felicity knew where they were. Looking down, she saw the three outer Gray Gulls knee-deep in the shallow sea. It was low tide. The gully would be uncovered now, but they were too far from the edge of the cliff to see it from here. A sign on the fence warned

them against going any nearer: DANGER. DO NOT GO BE-
YOND THIS POINT. PENALTY £50.

"This is where he usually comes," Bony said. "He
leans against this post and stares out to sea. For ages."

Felicity shrugged. "It's a nice view."

"He stands with the wind flapping his shirt, but he
never coughs. Not once. Odd, isn't it?"

"Sea air's healthy. Everyone knows that."

"He doesn't limp, either, when there's nobody there
to watch him. Is that the sea air too?"

"How do you know what he does when there's nobody there?" Felicity asked, laughing. "You're not nobody. Or are you invisible?"

"I'm behind that bush," Bony said, pointing.

She stared at him. "You're mad. Raving mad. You
want your head examined. How long have you been
following him around, crouching behind bushes while
he admires the view? Poor Bony, all that trouble for
nothing."

"Not nothing," he said, and took a small notebook out
of his pocket. "Do you want to hear what I've found
out?"

She looked at him uneasily, and then at the notebook
in his hands, uncertain whether she really wanted to
hear. It seemed disloyal to Mr. Ross. But her curiosity
overcame her, and when Bony sat down on the short
turf, she came and sat beside him.

"All right. What?" she asked in the tone of voice of
someone who was prepared to disbelieve every word.

"He's been here well over three weeks now," Bony

said, "and he hasn't received one letter in all that time. Not from India. Not from anywhere."

"How do you know?"

"I asked your mother."

"When?"

"The other day. I met her in the paper shop."

"Oh." Felicity was silent, remembering her mother telling her that she'd feel happier if something actually arrived: his money, his trunks, a letter, anything.

"Don't you think that's odd?" Bony asked.

"No. I haven't had a letter for ages, either. It doesn't make me a criminal."

"That's different," Bony said impatiently. "You belong here. Why should anyone write to you? It's not your birthday. But he's supposed to be waiting for his money, and he hasn't even posted any letters. Or made any telephone calls—"

"That's not true," Felicity said, interrupting angrily. "He has made a telephone call. Dad said so. He rang up his agent in India—"

"Not from the Fairweather," Bony said. "I asked your mother. And not from the post office. I asked Mrs. Farrington. He hasn't bought any stamps, either."

"She couldn't possibly remember—"

"Yes, she could. She knows Mr. Ross. She brought round the clothes for him from the Women's Guild, remember. She said she'd been looking out for him, but he never came."

Felicity got up and kicked at a stone angrily, watching it bounce and leap down the path toward Gull Bay. That was the trouble with living in a small town. Everyone knew everyone else's business. The tide of summer visitors flowed in and out, and they were easily forgotten from one season to another. But Mr. Ross was different. He was marked out because she, a local girl, had saved him from the Gray Gulls. The whole town had wanted a share in the excitement. The Women's Guild had collected clothing for the poor stranger who'd lost everything in their sea. The Charity ladies had given him money, although only as a loan. Mr. Ross had become as much their good deed as hers. They were proud of their generosity. There was no way he could walk into the small branch post office unnoticed. Especially not wearing Mr. Farrington's old jacket and Harry Benson's trousers.

"Gullington," she said. "He could've gone into Gullington."

Bony shook his head. "I thought of that. Nobody remembers him on the bus. Nobody remembers seeing him waiting at the stop. I didn't ask the drivers," he admitted fairly. "I thought it might seem a little odd."

"Odd," she repeated, staring at him. "What about—" She snatched the book out of his hands and saw the list of names: Mrs. Farrington, Miss Epsom, Mrs. Markes, Mrs. Dewson, Mr. Matthews, and dozens more. They were all there, all the gossips of Gull Bay, with their watching eyes and wagging tongues. "Do you know what you've done, Bony? Do you know what you've done?" she demanded hysterically.

"Nothing," he said defensively, startled by the fury in her voice. "I don't know what you mean. I only asked a few questions."

"A few questions! You know what they're like!"

She looked back toward Gull Bay. The small town was almost hidden by a clump of trees. She could only just see the smudge of roofs bordering Hycliffe Road and the top of St. Peter's tower. A faint gray haze seemed to hang over it, like the breath of gossip poisoning the air.

She knew what they were like—what she herself was like, she thought guiltily, remembering what Miss Pepper had said. But at least she had only made up stories about the summer visitors who came and went and did not have to live here, like her poor old dad.

She remembered what they'd said about him when his wine bar had folded, the little groups falling silent when they caught sight of her, but not before she'd heard the sly remarks. "It's the family I'm sorry for." "They say he drinks like a fish." "They say Mrs. Tait won't let him help in the guest house, in case . . ."

It wasn't true! Dad had never come rolling home drunk in his life. His face was naturally red and cheerful, and he liked to sing occasionally as he strolled home in the evenings—what was wrong with that?

But it hadn't stopped the town from talking. And they wouldn't stop talking about Mr. Ross, a stranger without a friend to speak up for him, except for her, Felicity Tait, who was well known for breaking everything she touched.

"You've done it now!" she cried, turning on Bony furiously. "He's weak and ill, and you set out deliberately to turn everyone against him, you and your stupid questions! You didn't even have the courage to accuse him to his face—oh, no. You went sneaking about behind his back. Out of spite. Just because he knew more about India than you do. You've spoiled it all. You've spoiled the only good thing I ever did. I—I—"

She put her hand to her mouth and bit her knuckle, afraid that she was going to cry with grief and rage.

Bony stood up slowly. He took the notebook from her and put it back in his pocket. "It wasn't because of India," he said. "Honestly. There is something fishy about him, I know there is. It's so obvious—I don't know what's the matter with you all. He seems to have got you under a sort of spell. Even Miss Pepper now."

"Miss Pepper?"

"She wasn't so keen on him at first. D'you know what I heard her call him? The young man of the sea. I didn't know what she meant, till Mum said yesterday she hoped Mr. Ross wouldn't turn out to be an old man of the sea. You're good at English. Do you know who the old man of the sea was?"

Felicity did not answer but turned away abruptly and began walking quickly down the path. He caught up with her.

"It's from one of the Sinbad stories," he told her. "I looked it up. Sinbad sees this poor old man wanting to cross a creek—a gully, Fliss, just like ours down there. So he takes pity on him and carries him across. But then he's stuck with him. The old man won't get off his back. He turns Sinbad into a slave. . . ."

The wind seemed colder . . . a cold wind, a sky as dark as midnight, a wet arm over her shoulders like an iron yoke. Felicity shivered and pushed the memory away, coming back into the hot sunlight, the rough path, and the heavy scent of gorse. She turned on Bony.

"Go away!" she said, wanting to hurt him. "Go and play with your bones, fat boy!"

But he wouldn't leave her alone. "I've made up another limerick," he said, jogging up and down by her side. "D'you want to hear it?"

"No."

"It's about you and Mr. Ross. About that silver gull brooch you keep wearing—know what it is? It's the mark of a slave. That's what he's turned you into, his little slave."

She ignored him and walked more quickly, but it was no good. He ran beside her, chanting mockingly:

> "That smiling young man of the sea
> Is not what you think him to be.
> He's gulled you and caught you,
> With silver he's bought you
> And now you will never be free."

Felicity clenched her fists but kept silent.

"He didn't even buy it himself," Bony said. "Miss Tatterson got it for him."

Let Bony think what he liked. It had nothing to do with him. She knew her silence was annoying him, and she was glad.

"I suppose you think he told her what to get? Well, he didn't. He just asked her to get a little present for you. Nothing too expensive, he said. Anything suitable for a child."

"Liar!" she said, turning to face him. "Liar! Liar! Liar!"

"Ask Miss Peacock. She told me. It came from her shop. Miss Tatterson asked her to suggest something cheap and showy—"

Felicity hit him. Her fist struck his cheek, leaving a white mark that turned red as his face grew pale.

They stood, staring at each another.

Then Bony said, his voice shaking, "That's right. Hit me. You're quite safe. I won't hit back. I'm a pacifist. Anyone can hit me. Even a girl. Even a friend. Go on, hit me again. Help yourself." He stood in front of her, turning his other cheek, looking both absurd and oddly heroic.

"Oh, don't be silly," she said, turning away, sick at herself. "I didn't hit you hard."

"Try again, then," he said. "You never know your luck. You might knock me over the cliff."

"Go away!" she shouted. "Leave me alone. I hate you. I never want to see you again."

"Very well," he said, after a pause. "That's it. That's the end." And he walked away.

She watched him go. The wind blew her hair about her head and whispered through the gorse. "This is the parting way, this is the end . . ."

She stood for a long time, thinking. Then she unpinned the silver gull from her shirt and threw it as hard as she could toward the edge of the cliff. The wind caught it, and for a moment it seemed to hang in the air, glittering in the sunlight. Then it was gone.

Chapter 15

Bony marched angrily down the cliff path, making up a new limerick in his head. It wasn't one of his best, but it gave him considerable satisfaction, and he muttered it under his breath all the way home.

> A person I thoroughly hate
> Is a girl called Felicity Tait.
> Her brain is so small,
> She can't reason at all,
> So she uses her fists in debate.

Back in his room, he examined his face carefully in the mirror. His cheeks were their normal color again, and however hard he peered, he could see no sign of a bruise. Pity. She hadn't hit him hard enough. Couldn't even do that properly.

If I'd hit her, she'd have a black eye, all right, he thought. *She'd have been pulverized.*

He clenched his fist and admired the bulge of muscle

in his arm. He wasn't fat, just well built. Sturdy. Helping Dad move heavy furniture about had developed his strength. He bet he could flatten any boy in his grade if he wanted to. But he did not want to. What was the point? It wouldn't solve anything.

"It takes more courage to be a pacifist," he told his reflection, and his reflection nodded a little ruefully, agreeing with him but knowing how difficult this was to prove, even to himself.

If only I had a chance to do something really brave, he thought. *If only I had been the one to rescue Mr. Ross.* . . .

He frowned. Was he jealous of Felicity? Had he disliked Mr. Ross simply because the man hadn't waited to be rescued on another day when Bony, himself, happened to be walking by?

No. That was absurd. He'd had good reasons. . . .

Bony took his notebook out of his pocket and turned the pages uneasily. What did his carefully accumulated evidence really prove? Nothing very much. He had not been able to follow Mr. Ross every minute of the day. The man could have posted a dozen letters unseen, telephoned from a dozen kiosks. His limp and cough might be merely nervous habits, brought on by people staring at him. Like Watson, their cat, who'd gone on limping long after the vet had said his injured leg was cured.

How can I be sure? Bony wondered gloomily.

He walked over to his collection of bones. The sight of them pleased him. Bones were facts; solid, uncomplicated. You could label them—

One had no label. Frowning, he picked up the seabird's skull. Odd sort of beak. Distinctive. "Can't be an albatross, though," he'd told Felicity sternly. "My book says they fly round the southern oceans. And that's ten thousand miles away, at the bottom of the world. Right down there, see?"

"No wonder he was so tired when he came," she'd said.

Daft girl. Her mind did not work like other people's; it just played around. Even she could not really believe the man was a bird. True, there was something oddly birdlike about his round, bright eyes . . . something strange . . .

Bony put the skull back on the table, suddenly dissatisfied with his collection. He wanted to know more than the bones could tell him. He wanted to know what went on in a living head.

Mrs. White was still in the shop, which did not close till late during the season. Bony, glancing in, saw she was trying to sell a small, decorated box to two summer visitors. She frowned him away, and he shut the door quietly. Dad was out, delivering a chest of drawers to a house on the other side of Gullington. Bony felt restless. He went into the kitchen, helped himself to some biscuits, and took them out with him, eating them in the street as he made his way to the seafront.

He saw some boys he knew in the distance but made no attempt to catch up with them. He did not want to talk. He wanted to think.

There was nothing wrong with asking questions, was there?

His father, whom he admired, had always encouraged him to.

"Anything you want to know, just ask," he'd said. "Don't be ashamed to confess ignorance. We're not born knowing everything. We all have to find things out, and the best way is by asking."

His mother, on the other hand, seemed to hold a different view.

"You shouldn't have asked Mrs. Benson her age, Sam. You should never ask a woman her age. It's rude," she'd said, and on another occasion: "You shouldn't have asked Mr. Jefferson how much he earns. It's none of your business."

"But I wanted to know."

"You want to know too much," his mother had said.

"Don't take things for granted," Mr. Pearson at school had told them. "Question everything."

Bony wished they'd make up their minds.

Resting his arms on the railings, he looked down into the bay. Most of the summer visitors had gone for their supper. There were only a few people about. Two youths were pulling a rubber dinghy out of the water, and Mrs. Farrington was walking her dog.

The sea was on its long way in, licking at abandoned sand castles as if they were so many ice creams. A small boy, kneeling beside his decorated fortress, was shoveling sand onto its ramparts in a desperate attempt to keep the sea away. Beside him, his mother yawned and looked at her watch. A tall, thin man, his pale hair blowing in the wind, was walking slowly toward the steps in the seawall. Mr. Ross.

He looked different. For one thing, he was not limping. Also, his pale skin had been reddened by the sun, giving him a glow of health. There was nothing left of the weak, white-faced invalid. Bony stared.

He was not the only one watching Mr. Ross come lightly up the steps. Two local women, standing a few yards away on the promenade, were also looking at him out of the corners of their sharp eyes. They were talking together in low voices, their heads almost touching.

Bony could not hear what they were saying, but he did not need to. Their sly, avid faces told him enough. Felicity had been right. His questions had set the town gossiping.

"You didn't even have the courage to accuse him to his face," she'd said. That had hurt more than the blow on his cheek. She thought he was a coward . . . and perhaps it was true.

Mr. Ross had passed the two gossips now and was coming toward him. He hadn't noticed Bony. He was throwing a pebble up into the air and catching it again. He looked happy. Behind him, the two women began whispering again, their eyes sharp on his defenseless back.

You didn't even have the courage to accuse him to his face!

Bony stepped forward. "Can I have a word with you, Mr. Ross?" he asked.

Chapter 16

They sat side by side on a bench in the small park overlooking the promenade. Some distance away, a gardener was sweeping up litter from the paths. There was no one else about. The roses in the flower beds were overblown, and the sun was low in the sky, casting long shadows.

It was a good place for a confidential talk with a man you did not trust, which was why Bony had chosen it. There were people within shouting distance but no one near enough to hear what they said, if they kept their voices down.

So far, however, not a word had been spoken. Bony found it difficult to begin. It's hard to call someone a liar and a fraud in cold blood. He wished Mr. Ross would say something to annoy him so that he could lose his temper. It would be easier then. But Mr. Ross seemed perfectly content to wait in silence. He was gently rotating his weak ankle and gazing down at it thoughtfully.

"It's better now, isn't it?" Bony asked.

"Yes. Much better, thank you," Mr. Ross said politely.

"You look better too. Your face is quite red now."

"I've caught the sun—"

"How come you missed it in India?" Bony asked, seeing his chance. "The sun's much hotter there. I've been stupid. I should've seen it right away. Your face was as white as a bone when you came here—and don't tell me it was because you've been ill!" he added before Mr. Ross had a chance to speak, "because I won't believe you!"

"Why not?" Mr. Ross asked. He had turned to look at Bony, but his voice expressed only mild interest.

"Because sunburn doesn't fade as quickly as all that. You'd have been sallow, not dead white—"

"Supposing I'd worn a hat all the time?" Mr. Ross asked hopefully.

Bony could have hit him.

"I suppose you think that's funny?" he said furiously. "You think I'm a joke, don't you? You imagine that because I'm a kid, it doesn't matter what I say. Well, it does. You'll find out. The whole town's talking about you now—and it was me who started them off!"

"What are they saying?"

"They think you're a liar. They don't believe you've ever been to India. And nor do I," Bony added defiantly.

To his surprise Mr. Ross laughed. "Oh, well, I suppose it couldn't last forever," he said. "You're quite right. I'm afraid I'm a terrible liar. I've never been to India in my life."

Bony was so taken aback by this easy admission that for a moment he could only stare at Mr. Ross. The man looked back at him quite calmly, neither angry nor afraid.

"Then why did you say you had?" Bony asked at last.

"Oh, I don't know." Mr. Ross spread his hands helplessly. "I just drifted into it. . . . The first morning, Felicity looked so young and hopeful, as if she longed for amazing things, a little magic somewhere. I didn't want her to be disappointed in me. So I told her what I thought would please her. I always like to please people. And I enjoy telling stories, don't you?"

"I prefer facts," Bony said coldly. He had a horrid feeling that the man was slipping through his fingers again. He couldn't even see him clearly. The sun was shining in his eyes. "I can see it might have begun as a sort of joke, but you kept it up—"

"It kept itself up," Mr. Ross said eagerly. "It seemed to gather momentum . . . suddenly I found everyone believed I was a great explorer. They began to make up their own stories about me—China, India, Japan, there was nowhere I hadn't been. Nothing I had not done. And remember, I was weak and tired. I needed somewhere to rest. So I let myself be carried along. And fed. Besides, I'd always wanted to go to India," he added, as if in excuse. "I've often dreamed of it. So it wasn't exactly a lie, was it?"

"Yes," Bony said, astonished. "Of course it was."

"But they all wanted to believe me. Don't you think it would be a pity to disillusion them now?"

"No," Bony said stubbornly, amazed at the man's effrontery. "I think you should tell them the truth. Or I will."

"The truth," Mr. Ross said, and sighed. "I'm afraid I don't always know what that is."

"You must know what you are!" Bony said angrily, and was furious when Mr. Ross laughed.

"I'm sorry," Mr. Ross said, apologizing quickly, "but you make it sound so simple, and it's really much more difficult than that, isn't it?" he added.

Bony remembered his own doubts about himself and flushed.

But that was different. He intended to find out, one way or another. He wasn't going to hide behind a lot of fluffy daydreams. If he was a coward, well, he'd admit it. It wouldn't be the end of the world.

"So you think I should own up?" Mr. Ross asked, interrupting these thoughts.

"Yes."

"Perhaps you're right." Mr. Ross stood up and glanced at the sky. "It's time for me to go," he said, and began to walk away.

Bony hurried after him. "What are you going to do? What are you going to say?" he demanded. "What are you going to tell them?"

"Don't worry. I expect I'll think of something," Mr. Ross said absently. He was looking at the people on the promenade ahead of them.

"What d'you mean, *think* of something?" Bony said indignantly. "You've got to tell them the truth!"

But Mr. Ross was no longer listening to him. He was waving to someone. Red hair. Miss Pepper.

"Excuse me, Bony," he said politely, and went to meet her.

"Are you going to tell them?" Bony shouted after him.

"Yes," Mr. Ross said, looking back.

"When?"

"Tonight."

Bony stared after him, uncertain whether to believe him or not. Mr. Ross had greeted Miss Pepper, who was showing him some yellow leaflets. Now they were walking back toward the Fairweather. He began to follow them, then stopped, remembering he'd quarreled with Felicity. Pity. He'd have liked to be there when Mr. Ross confessed he was a liar. He'd love to see Felicity's face—no. Perhaps not.

She wasn't going to thank him for what he'd done, he realized uneasily, and for the first time he began to wish he'd let things alone.

Chapter 17

Felicity hung over the banisters, looking down into the hall. She was waiting for Mr. Ross to come in. She wanted to see if he'd look any different to her, now that she was no longer wearing his silver brooch. The mark of a slave, Bony had called it. Well, she wasn't going to be anybody's slave. The little silver gull was now at the bottom of the sea. Good riddance to it. Mr. Ross was a cheat and a liar—and she had helped him tell his lies.

"I must have been crazy," she muttered.

"What are you mumbling about?" her sister asked, startling Felicity.

"I thought you were out," she said, turning round.

"I'm going out soon. I'm just getting ready," Susan said, and added, unable to contain her delight, "Timmy Barnes is taking me to see that new film in Gullington."

Timmy Barnes? So that was why she was no longer playing sad records in her room. She'd gotten a new boyfriend and a new happy face to go with him. A great improvement.

"Good for you," Felicity said.

"Your turn will come in time," Susan said kindly, spoiling it by giving Felicity a quick, critical look. Felicity guessed what she was thinking. Too tall. Too skinny. Like a lamppost.

"Is Mum in?" she asked as Susan turned to go back into her room.

"Yes. She's in the kitchen."

"Is she in a good temper?"

"Why? What have you done now?" Susan asked, turning round to look at her. "For heaven's sake, don't upset her before I've gone. Hide. Keep out of her way. Let me get out of the house first."

"I haven't done anything," Felicity said. "Yet."

"What do you mean?"

"I just wanted to tell her something—"

"Well, I wouldn't. Not now. Leave it till tomorrow," Susan said, leaning forward to inspect herself in the mirror.

"What's she cross about? Me?"

"No, not this time. I think someone on the Charity Committee said something to upset her. They had a special meeting here this afternoon."

"What about?"

Susan glanced at her but did not answer. Instead she stood up quickly, looked once more in the mirror and then at her watch, and went to the door.

"What was it about, Susan?"

Susan hesitated. Then she said, "It was about your Mr. Ross. They want to know when he's going to pay back the money they loaned him. They hinted things.

. . . Mum's really wild, Fliss. I'd keep out of her way if I were you."

Mrs. Tait was in the kitchen, slicing ham for the guests' evening meal with a thin, very sharp knife. Felicity watched her.

"Don't jog the table, dear."

"I'm not."

"Well, please don't stand so near me. You make me nervous."

Felicity stepped back obediently. Her mother looked angry. Her face was flushed, and every now and then her lips moved soundlessly, as if she were carrying on a silent quarrel, saying all the cutting things she had not thought of in time.

Perhaps Susan was right, Felicity thought, *I'd better leave it.*

"Is Dad in?" she asked.

"Not yet. He had an interview in Gullington."

"Perhaps he's got the job."

"Perhaps," Mrs. Tait said. "Perhaps pigs will fly."

Poor Dad, Felicity thought.

But then her mother said suddenly, "No. No, I'm being unfair. He does his best. I'm sorry, dear. I don't mean to be horrid. It's just . . . those wretched women upset me."

"I expect you're tired," Felicity said, trying to hide her surprise at this unexpected apology. Her mother's face looked strangely soft, uncertain. "Can I help you, Mum?" she asked.

"Thank you, dear. You can cut those tomatoes into quarters if you like. Only, be careful of your fingers."

For a moment they worked in friendly silence, for once at ease with each other. Then they both glanced toward the door, which Felicity had not shut properly. They heard voices in the hall. Miss Pepper and Mr. Ross were back.

Felicity looked quickly at her mother, but Mrs. Tait's face was expressionless, and she went on cutting cucumber without saying anything. The voices in the hall died away. Someone laughed in the distance.

The sound of it infuriated Felicity. She thought she knew who was laughing. How he must have been laughing at them all the time.

"Are you going to have a talk with Mr. Ross tonight?" she asked quickly.

"No," Mrs. Tait said, "I'm not."

Felicity stared at her. It was not the answer she'd expected. Not the answer she wanted.

"I think you ought to, Mum," she said. "I think you should tell him to go."

As her mother looked up at her in surprise, she felt herself flushing. She'd done it now. She'd betrayed Mr. Ross.

"Oh, you do, do you?" her mother said, "Well, this is a turnabout. Only this morning you were begging me to let him stay, and now you can't wait for him to go. I suppose that's Susan's doing. I knew she was listening. Well, let me tell you something, miss. Nobody's going to dictate to me. If I choose to give someone free board and lodging, that's my business."

"Mum, he's a liar! He's never been to India—"

"And how do you know that, pray?"

"Someone told me," Felicity said, not wanting to give Bony away. "Everyone says we're stupid to let him stay. Everybody's talking—"

"I know everybody's talking. I've had a bellyful of their talking this afternoon," Mrs. Tait said, the inelegant word sounding odd in her soft-spoken anger. Even now she remembered the possibly listening guests and shut the door firmly before continuing. This mixture of fury and control was rather frightening. Felicity kept quiet.

"Nothing better to do than spend their time gossiping," her mother went on. "First it's about your poor father, and now it's about this harmless young man. It's no thanks to the council that he didn't drown. If I've told them once, I've told them a hundred times to put up better warning notices. If you ask me, they owe him something. Let them talk. They'll not make up my mind for me, thank you very much. I take people as I find them."

She stopped for breath, and Felicity stared at her in astonishment, hardly able to believe that her attempt to betray Mr. Ross had gone so ridiculously wrong.

"And you know what they'd say if I did turn him out, don't you?" her mother asked. "Oh, they'd change their tune quick enough. Then I'd figure as a heartless, money-grubbing landlady who'd send a young man out to die in the cold rather than forgo her rent—"

"It's not cold."

"Oh, you know what I mean," her mother said irritably. "They don't like me. I don't know why, I'm sure. I've always done my best for the town. Given up my time—and money. Always been willing to help with advice. But it's no good. They just don't like me." She turned away and, with fingers that shook a little, began putting plastic wrap over a plate of ham.

Felicity did not know what to say. She knew it was true but had not realized that her mother knew it too. Poor Mum, who was so brisk and capable and perfect that she couldn't help criticizing everybody else. Felicity got up and hugged her awkwardly, nearly making her mother drop the plate of ham.

Her mother smiled and sniffed and said Felicity wasn't to take any notice of her, she was being a fool. Then she said, with a helplessness Felicity had never seen in her before, "What am I going to do about Mr. Ross? They want their money back. *I* can't afford to give it to them. What am I going to do?"

"Ask Dad."

"Your father wouldn't be any help," her mother said with the slight contempt that was often in her voice nowadays when she spoke of him.

"You've been listening to the gossip about Dad. You've begun to believe it yourself."

Her mother stared at her and flushed crimson.

"Give Dad a chance, Mum," Felicity said.

Mrs. Tait turned away sharply and went over to the sink where she stood not really doing anything, just moving pans about with sharp clicks and clatters. Then she said, without looking round, "All right. I will."

Chapter 18

Felicity helped her mother serve the guests their cold ham salad, keeping well away from the table by the window, where Mr. Ross sat. Then she slipped out to wait on the front steps for her father to come home.

She wanted to get at him before he saw her mother, to warn him to be—what? Masterful, brisk, efficient? More like Mum, in fact? No. She did not really want him to change. She liked him as he was, easygoing and soft.

He came back, rosy and smiling, and smelling delicately of whiskey.

"Dad! You've been drinking. Haven't you got a peppermint?"

"Really, Felicity," he said, then, seeing her glance toward the kitchen, smiled ruefully. "Stormy weather, is it? I know I'm late. Never mind. Your mother won't be cross with me tonight. I've good news. I'm being considered for that job at Rickman's."

"Oh, Dad!"

"Don't get too excited. It probably won't come to anything," he said quickly, too used to disappointment to trust his luck any longer. "Let's go and tell her—"

"Not yet! Dad, something's happened," Felicity said, clinging to his arm.

"Can't it wait?"

"No," she said, and told him everything about Mr. Ross—the bird chart and Bony's notebook, the disappearing limp, the lack of letters and telephone calls. All she left out were the books on India, finding them too difficult to explain.

Her father listened impatiently. He wanted to go and tell Mum about the job. He wanted to have his supper in front of the television, with Fiddles on his lap and a glass of whiskey in his hand. The last thing he wanted was to get involved in all this taradiddle.

"Really, Fliss," he said. "Albert Ross, albatross, indeed! I suppose you think young Kitty Wake at the Red Lion is a master criminal, just because her parents liked puns. I've never heard such nonsense."

"Dad, please do something. Mum's worried."

"Oh, very well," he said easily. "Just leave it to me."

But as she followed him into the kitchen, she could not help remembering all the other times he had said, "Leave it to me," and done nothing. The garden gate still hung by one hinge, the window in the outside toilet was still cracked, the cold tap in one of the bathrooms still dripped.

His interview at Rickman's had to be discussed first. It was not until he'd finished his supper that he said, "Now, what's all this about Mr. Ross?"

"It's the Charity Committee, Ben," Mrs. Tait said. "They want their money back."

"They'll just have to wait. What do they expect the poor devil to do? Swim out to India to fetch it?"

"Dad—" Felicity began.

He looked at her. "Yes, I know. You and that fat boy playing detective all over the place. Concocting wild stories—"

"What's this?" Mrs. Tait said sharply. "Felicity, what have you been up to?"

"Nothing!"

"Just a game," Mr. Tait said quickly, realizing too late that Felicity had not told her mother everything. "It's not important. You don't happen to know what won the two-thirty, do you?" he asked, picking up a newspaper.

"So you won't have a word with Mr. Ross?" Mrs. Tait said wearily, as if she'd always known she could not count on him to do anything even mildly unpleasant.

"Dad, please—"

"All right, all right," he said, putting the paper down. "Can't have our young daughter worried, can we? Where is he? In his room? I'll go along now and shake the truth out of him. You leave him to me."

Felicity and her mother looked at him doubtfully, knowing how easygoing he was, suspecting he'd take a bottle of wine with him and that he and Mr. Ross would end up singing sea chanties to the moon.

They were wrong. There was no sound of singing from the garden room. Felicity, watching from the shadow of the viburnum bush, saw her father's silhou-

ette on the thin curtain of the lighted window. Tall and
upright and impressive. She could not see Mr. Ross. She
imagined him sitting on his bed in the ill-fitting clothes
the town had given him, looking like an orphan boy
with his thin face and fair, ragged hair.

She crept nearer, but she could only hear the sound of
their voices, not what they were saying. The wind was
too loud in the trees, tossing the branches until they
sounded like wild wings beating. The words of the
poem came back to her:

> With his cruel bow he laid full low
> The harmless Albatross.

Her mind began to fill with superstitious terrors. She
stood, trembling in the evening wind, telling herself not
to be so stupid. Mr. Ross was not a bird of doom. Nothing terrible would happen because she had brought him
down. The sea would not boil and bubble in the bay,
nor would slimy monsters rise from its depths. . . .
How Bony would laugh if she told him! He would not
give her a chance. He'd walk away if he saw her coming. He'd never tease her again.

"So that's where you are," her mother whispered. "I
might have known. Come into the house this minute."

Back in their shabby, familiar room, they were silent
at first, each thinking her own thoughts. Then Mrs.
Tait said, "I refuse to believe he's been deceiving us all
this time. Not him. He has such—such an innocent
look. Like a child's."

Felicity wondered which child her mother could pos-

sibly be thinking of. Nobody in Gull Bay, that was for
sure.

"I'm sure he'll be able to explain everything satisfac-
torily," her mother said next. "You'll see. I expect his
money will arrive tomorrow, and we'll wonder what
we were making a fuss about. And won't I enjoy telling
the committee," she added, smiling happily, lost in this
delightful daydream.

Felicity looked at her with pity, finding her mother's
hopes even more fantastic than her own fears.

"Mum, he's a liar," she said as her father opened the
door.

"I'm afraid you're right," he said.

They turned to stare at him, and he made a rueful
face. He looked exhausted.

"Yes. We can stop looking through the post for a letter from India. There won't be one. It was all a pack of
lies."

"Oh, no! Oh, no, Ben!" Mrs. Tait cried. She put her
hands up to her head as if to hold it on. "The money!
The money they loaned him! How are we going to pay
it back? How can I face them?"

"Don't worry." Mr. Tait took an envelope from his
pocket and threw it onto the table. "It's all there. He
hasn't touched a penny of it. In fact, he insisted on giving it to me. I think he was afraid he might be tempted
to spend it otherwise. 'I'm not a thief,' he kept saying. 'I
only take what I'm given freely.' Poor young devil. You
don't have to check it," he added irritably as Mrs. Tait
began to count the money.

"Five, six, seven," she muttered, ignoring him.

Mr. Tait sighed, walked heavily across the room, and slumped down into his chair. His normally cheerful face looked gray and sad.

"What did you say to him, Dad?" Felicity asked. "Was it horrid? Did you have to force him to confess?"

"Third degree, you mean? Really, Fliss, what do you think I am? No. No, it was all too easy. He didn't try to deny anything, he simply . . . collapsed. He told me everything. I think he was glad to get it all out." He paused and then said slowly, "He's a strange young man. I can't help wondering if he's a bit simple."

"Why?"

"Oh, I don't know. He just doesn't seem to know his way around. I asked him what benefit he was entitled to, and he didn't seem to know what I was talking about."

For a moment there was silence in the room, except for the mutter of Mrs. Tait's counting. "Thirty-eight, thirty-nine, forty . . ."

"Poor Mr. Ross," Felicity said sadly.

"Poor Mr. Ross indeed!" her mother cried angrily. "What about us? He's made us look like fools. The whole town will be laughing at us. I can just hear them—" She broke off with a harsh breath, almost a sob. Then she looked down at the notes in her hand. "Where was I?"

"Forty," Felicity said.

"Forty-one, forty-two, forty-three . . . I suppose he's penniless, then?"

"Yes."

"I might have known it. And unemployed?"

"There's no shame in being unemployed," Mr. Tait said sharply. "It can happen to the best of us. And so I told him."

Felicity looked at her mother, who flushed and went back to counting the money.

"What's going to happen to him, Dad?" Felicity asked.

Before her father could answer, her mother looked up and said bitterly, "Need you ask? We're going to keep him, of course. I'm sure your father told him he could stay. Didn't you, Ben?"

"Yes, I did. What did you expect me to do? Throw him out into the street? That's what *he* expected, poor devil. That's why he told us all those lies. He was frightened we'd turn him out if he told the truth. Oh, he hasn't any illusions about charity. Do you know what he said? That there's always a limit to kindness. He said people are afraid to take misfortune into their home, in case it has come to stay."

"That's all very fine," Mrs. Tait said, her voice shaking. "He's not at a loss for words, I must say. A limit to kindness—what does he expect? An easy ride through life on our backs? We've enough troubles of our own, thank you. He should stand on his own two feet."

"He's got a bad ankle," Felicity said, before she could stop herself. It was the sort of remark that, though true, always annoyed her mother. It did now.

"You were the one who wanted me to tell him to go," she pointed out. "Have you changed your mind again?"

"I—I don't know."

It was true. She did not know what she wanted, nor

whose side she was on any longer. Perhaps there was a limit to kindness. Gran had thought so. Though she had persuaded Mum to let them keep Fiddles, when he'd turned up as a bedraggled kitten, all spiky fur and bones, she had shut the door firmly after him. "No more," she'd said. "The world is full of strays. We can't take them all in. It's somebody else's turn now."

Perhaps it was somebody else's turn for Mr. Ross. But supposing nobody would take him in?

"I'm sorry," Felicity said. "It's my fault. I brought him here."

They looked at her in surprise.

Then her father laughed and hugged her. "Your fault, indeed! You're my hero. It'd be a poor world if we let people drown in case they turned out to be a nuisance. What an idea!"

"You're making me ashamed of myself," Mrs. Tait said. She took Felicity's hand and smiled at her. "I didn't mean . . . I wasn't cross with you, dear. I'm proud of you. We both are. You should hear me boasting to the committee about my wonderful daughter—" She broke off, then went on bravely. "Oh, well, let them laugh at me. I'm sure I don't care. Your father's right. We can't turn Mr. Ross out now. Not until he has somewhere to go. But there's no reason why he shouldn't pay something toward his bed and board. He must be entitled to some sort of benefit— There I go. Money again. But someone has to think of it." She sighed and said wistfully, "You know, he thought I was kind, he kept telling me I was so kind. . . . I'm not, really, and I know it. I'm too impatient. But I did try. I thought perhaps I could change, become a nicer person. . . . But it was all lies, of course."

"It wasn't, Mum," Felicity said eagerly. "You are a bit nicer. I've noticed it myself. I could see you trying not to be cross with me—"

Her mother laughed. "You'll have to help me, Felicity," she said.

Felicity lay in bed, thinking. It wasn't her fault. It was just her luck. If anyone else had saved a man from the sea, he'd have turned out to be a millionaire or a film star or, at the very least, an ordinary citizen who would thank them, shake their hands, and walk away.

Only she would fish out a penniless weakling, who told lies and might not, for all they knew, be telling the whole truth now. Only she would saddle her family with a young man of the sea and dream he was a silver bird, bringing good luck to all who were kind to him. She was back to being the old Felicity again, the girl who had only to touch something for it to come to pieces in her hands.

Chapter 19

Felicity awoke early. The night had changed nothing, yet somehow, while she slept, her tide of self-pity had ebbed away. The hard facts, like the beached Gray Gulls, had lost their power. The sun was shining.

"Don't cry over spilt milk," as Gran used to say. "You'll only spoil it for the cat."

Good advice. Gran had no patience with people who wallowed in misery. "I don't want your tears when I'm gone," she'd once told Felicity. "Dance on my grave if you like, but don't drizzle over it. I never could abide the damp."

Gran wouldn't have thought much of Mr. Ross, that was for sure. Like Miss Pepper, she distrusted charm. "What's he after?" she'd have demanded suspiciously. "Why doesn't he come right out with it? I can't stand wheedlers."

Poor Mr. Ross, Felicity thought, and shrugged. She wasn't going to cry over him today.

She was hungry. She sat up in bed and tried to guess

the time. It felt early. Too long to wait for breakfast. Getting up, she dressed quickly and went downstairs to raid the larder.

Mr. Ross was in the kitchen. Silhouetted against the window, the sun making a bright halo of his hair, his face in shadow, he looked again the mysterious stranger who'd appeared out of the sea spray.

She flushed scarlet, but he did not seem to notice her confusion.

"Hullo," he said, with one of the smiles she'd once thought he kept especially for her but now knew he gave to everyone, as freely as her mother's roses. "Isn't it a lovely day? Too good to waste indoors."

She walked forward till she could see him clearly. His face showed no sign of embarrassment or shame. His eyes, meeting hers, were bright and unclouded. She was the one who looked away.

"I'm just making some sandwiches," he said, though this was obvious. Buttered slices of bread, ham, and cucumber littered the table. "Your mother usually does them for me, but I thought as I was up early, I'd save her the trouble. I hope it's all right?"

"Yes, of course," she said politely.

It wasn't all right. Mum had been planning to have a serious talk with him that morning. Dad had wanted to take him round to the Welfare Department and get him sorted out. He had no right to take their food and go out for the day, as if he hadn't a care in the world.

"Would you like one?" he asked cheerfully. "Though perhaps you'd better not, if you're going swimming. I saw your friend Bony White setting off. Is he a good swimmer?"

"Bony? He can't swim at all."

"Oh? He had a towel under his arm, so I thought—"

"Where did you see him?" she said, interrupting him.

"Down in the bay. I'd gone to have a look at the sea, and I saw him walking across the sands toward the West cliffs. Perhaps he was just going to search for bones in the gully."

"He can't be! The tide's coming in." Felicity looked quickly at the clock. Five to seven. High tide was not till after nine, but already the sea would be approaching the gully, sending its cold, thin fingers through the tumbled stones.

"Are you worried?" Mr. Ross asked. "He struck me as a sensible boy. Not one to take silly risks."

"No," Felicity agreed. But she couldn't think what Bony was up to, going toward the West cliffs with a towel under his arm. "I think I'll go and look for him," she said.

"Shall I come with you?"

"No," she said decidedly. "You'd only hold me up, or break your leg or something."

It sounded rude, but he only smiled and waved her away.

"Good luck!" he called as she ran out of the room.

Bony White was sitting on the big boulder at the top of the rockfall. He was too early, of course. The sea had only just reached the mouth of the gully, and the rocks below him were only damp.

There was nobody in sight. He hadn't really expected there would be. Taking a sandwich out of a paper bag, he settled down to wait.

The waves washed in and out, slapped playfully at the stranded Gulls, and came sneaking up through the narrow channel. There was little force behind them now, but farther out, he could see the pattern of the strong currents quite plainly on the surface of the sea.

If he slipped while climbing down the rockfall when the tide was in, the sea would catch him and carry him away forever. And that would be the end of Bony White. No more summers or winters for him. All his hopes of fame and success thrown away. His parents' only child cracked like an egg on the Gray Gulls, in an attempt to prove to himself that he wasn't a coward.

What a waste! Pointless. If there'd been anyone there to be rescued, he'd have gone down like a shot. Wouldn't he?

He threw his apple core into the gully and watched a wave lick at it and draw back, as if not liking the taste. The sea was coming in more quickly now. Another half hour and it would be rushing through the gully, filling the air with its broken spray, making the rocks wet and treacherous underfoot. Would he have the courage to climb down then, as Felicity had done? If he didn't do it, he would never know. And he wanted to know. He always wanted to know.

He sighed and took a piece of cake from his bag. The condemned man ate a hearty breakfast . . .

The paper bag rustled suddenly. He put out his hand

to stop it from blowing off the boulder—and touched bare flesh. A foot. He looked up.

"You might offer me some cake," Felicity said, sitting down beside him.

"Why should I?" he demanded, cross with her for startling him. "Anyway, you owe me an apology."

"I apologize. I grovel," she said with a brilliant smile. "Now can I have some? I'm starving."

He handed her the bag but said reproachfully, "You hit me. Hitting a pacifist is . . . utterly despicable."

"Unfair," she agreed. "Like stealing pennies from a blind man."

He was not certain he liked the comparison. "I could've knocked your head off if I'd wanted to. Easily. It wouldn't have been much loss. You probably wouldn't even have missed it."

"I said I'm sorry."

She did not look in the least sorry. In fact, she looked remarkably happy, sitting in the misty sunlight munching his cake. It never occurred to him that she'd been afraid their friendship was over. He was loyal to his friends and never bore grudges for long. Instead he thought of Mr. Ross. The man couldn't have owned up last night. She wouldn't look so pleased with herself if he had.

"What are you doing here?" she asked. "The tide's coming in."

"I can see that."

"You're always telling us only a fool would come here when the tide's turned."

"I have my moments of folly," he said grandly.

She looked at him thoughtfully, and he felt uneasy, knowing her habit of making wild guesses, some of which, simply by the law of averages, were bound to be right.

"You've brought a towel," she observed, frowning. "You must've expected to get wet. . . ."

"Don't talk with your mouth full," he said, but she was not going to be put off so easily. He could almost see her imagination jumping about in her head before making its final leap onto the heights of absurdity.

"You were going to drown yourself!" she cried in alarm.

He burst out laughing.

"What's so funny about that?" she asked resentfully.

Unable to speak, he pointed to his towel.

"Oh," she said, and gave a reluctant smile. "All right, perhaps it wasn't that. Though you might've brought it as a bluff. Or for the coastguard to dry his hands on after he'd fished you out. Or—"

"You're an idiot."

"I'm beginning to think I am," she said with a sigh.

He looked at her in surprise. She was staring across the gully toward the rock on which Mr. Ross had been standing, looking as if she'd lost something important to her.

The sea was hurrying in, breaking against the Gray Gulls in a flurry of white feathers. He knew Felicity had woven her superstitions around them, as if they were malicious stone gods that had to be propitiated, bowed down to, and touched with crossed fingers. To him they were merely great lumps of inert matter, immovable objects against which the sea broke twice a day, patterning the sky with its foam.

"I used to think they were out to get me," Felicity said, "The Gulls, I mean. Silly, wasn't it? Kid's stuff," she added with a weary, rather grown-up smile.

"We are kids," he said, frowning.

He did not want Felicity to turn sensible on him. There was only room for one keen, scientific brain in their friendship. His. It always annoyed him that she sometimes got better marks than he did at school. It was her wild imagination he liked. Her supreme silliness.

"Shall I tell you my new limerick?" he asked.

"No," she said, as she always did.

And as always, he told her nonetheless.

> "Felicity Tait, I have heard
> That you think Albert Ross is a bird.
> But how can he fly
> Without wings in the sky?
> Aren't you being a little absurd?"

She smiled, but protested that she'd never thought he was a bird. "I just thought—oh, I don't know—that he was something free and strange and splendid. A traveler . . . You were right. He's a liar. He's never been to India." For a moment she looked puzzled, "Well, I sort of knew he hadn't, and yet—I suppose I still hoped he had."

"So he did own up," Bony said slowly, wondering if she knew his own part in it.

She didn't. "Dad got it out of him. You see, Mum was

worried because the committee cats had been getting at her." She told Bony what had happened, ending up with, "A proper old man of the sea he's turned out to be. Still, Mum says it's not my fault."

"Of course it isn't. It doesn't make any difference to what you did. You were brave," Bony said, and looked wistfully at the gully, wondering if he'd really have had the courage to do it. He'd never know now.

"I wasn't really," she confessed suddenly. "I was just in a hurry. You know me, I never stop to think. And I didn't even really save him. The stick broke. Why do things always have to break? It's enough to make me spit. So you see, I'm just as much a fake as he is. The sea did it, not me. It just spat him out at my feet."

"Even the sea didn't want him," Bony said, laughing. He noticed for the first time that she was no longer wearing the silver gull. She was cured. "He's not all that bad, really," he added, feeling generous now. "What's going to happen to him?"

"Mum and Dad are going to sort him out. Put some backbone into him. Set him to work. Mum doesn't see why he shouldn't do the washing up." She smiled and added, "He'll begin to wish he'd never come to the Fairweather."

"Poor Mr. Ross."

"Dad thinks he's a bit touched. Not crazy. You know, a bit missing up here." She tapped her forehead.

The gulls shrieked loudly, making a wild cacophony in the sky behind them. They turned and looked up.

Mr. Ross was standing on the edge of the cliff, looking down at them.

"*Go back!*" Felicity screamed frantically, as she had once before. "*Go back!*" and almost expected him to say, "I can't. It's even worse behind me now."

But he smiled and, giving an odd, beckoning wave, turned away. The ground sloped down from the edge of the cliff, and from where they were standing, it looked as if he were wading into the earth itself, knee-deep, waist-deep, and then he was out of sight.

"He was going to jump," Felicity whispered, looking terrified. "He was going to jump."

"Of course he wasn't," Bony said angrily. "Don't be stupid."

"But he must've climbed the fence—why should he climb the fence unless . . . d'you think he heard what we said?"

"No!"

"But the wind's blowing off the sea—"

"All right, supposing he did hear? So what? He wouldn't care what we think. We're only kids. We're not important to him, not even you. Lord, you must fancy yourself!" Bony spoke roughly. The sight of Mr. Ross poised on the cliff top had shocked him. Who could tell what might push that odd, weak creature over the edge? Gossip, perhaps, the gossip Bony himself had started with his questions. The shame of being found out, his glamour and his dreams stripped away, and unkind whispers following him wherever he went. . . .

"Come on," Bony said. "Hurry up!"

Without looking to see if she followed, he began running down the wide ledge, glancing frequently at the cliff as he did so. Somewhere between the gully and the bay he knew there was a way up. Some of the older boys at school claimed to have done it. "A difficult climb," they said. "Tricky. Don't you try it."

Bony did not have time to bother about that. All he worried about as he ran was how long Mr. Ross would wait before he looked over the edge once again and found his way was now clear.

Chapter 20

He did not want Felicity to come with him. It was his fault, not hers. As soon as the cliffs began to lean backward instead of forward, he tried to send her away. Pretended he had twisted his ankle. Began to limp heavily.

"You'd better run on or your mother'll get worried," he said. "You know what she is. I'll follow at my own pace."

She passed him with a sideways look. He thought he had gotten away with it when, to his fury, she stopped and looked up. "This is it," she said, and began to climb. He ran forward and tried to catch hold of her ankle, but she kicked out at him and scrambled out of reach. "I saw you looking for the way up," she said. "I'm not thick."

"Let me go first."

"No. If I slip, you can catch me, see?"

That was true, he thought, comforted. It was only fair to let her go first.

He began to climb after her. It was not as bad as he

had expected, more of a rough scramble than a climb. The youths must have exaggerated the danger to make themselves out to be heroes. The only trouble was that many of the rocks were loose.

"Test everything before you put your weight on it!" he shouted.

"I always do," she called back, and promptly dislodged a stone that hit him sharply on the head. "Sorry. That one didn't pass the test. You all right?"

He was about to tell her to be more careful but remembered in time that she'd once said it always made her break things. So he merely said, "Mind my head."

"I'll try, but it's difficult. There's so much loose stuff."

He looked up at her. She was moving lightly, easily, choosing her way with instinctive skill. It amazed him that people could call her clumsy. But for all her care, she could not help dislodging occasional showers of small stones that pattered over him like hail.

"Sorry," she'd call each time, looking down. She seemed to have no fear of heights.

The way was steeper now, and though the top of the cliff still looked far away, he knew they must be high up, for the sound of the sea in the gully was fainter now. He looked down and saw the spray bursting on the Gray Gulls far below. Then the whole world tilted, and the great rocks seemed to move as if about to take flight. Pressing himself against the cliff, he shut his eyes, and the darkness whirled and spun round inside his head.

He was going to faint. *Oh, please God, don't let me fall!*

He heard Felicity calling and opened his eyes. She had reached the top of the cliff and was lying flat on the grass, her head over the edge, looking down at him.

He knew she must see the sick terror on his face, but he could not move. His hands were clutching the rock so tightly that tremors began running up his arms, until the cliff itself seemed to vibrate, as if trying to shake him off.

"Come on, lazybones," she called. "Don't go to sleep. You're too fat, that's your trouble."

She was laughing at him. She had noticed nothing, except that he was slow. He closed his eyes again, glad that she would never know that he was a coward. When he fell to his death, she would only think it was because he was overweight.

Felicity knew perfectly well that Bony was frightened. His face was chalk-white, and she could practically hear his teeth rattle. He was standing with his stomach pressed so tightly to the cliff that the strain on his arms and legs must have been terrible.

Stupid fool, she thought angrily. He must've known he's got a bad head for heights. What did he have to do it for?

She was terrified he was going to fall.

She called down to him cheerfully, pretending she'd noticed nothing, hoping to make him relax. His eyes opened, and he looked up at her briefly before closing them once more.

She was about to climb down to help him when she noticed he was moving again. Upward. His eyes were still shut, and he was feeling for his holds, his fingers scrabbling on the rock. There was a look of blind determination on his poor, pea-green face, of dogged courage.

She hesitated. Bony was often teased at school because he would not fight. He hadn't seemed to care. But she'd heard the wistful note in his voice when he'd told her she'd been brave, and had known then what he'd been doing in the gully. He'd been going to test his courage by climbing down the rockfall when the tide was in.

The fat fool, she thought, sick with indecision and fear.

If she went to help him, he'd go on thinking himself a coward. God knew what stupid and dangerous tricks he'd get up to. Yet if she didn't, and he fell . . .

She wanted to shout down to him, "Let me do it for you! You'll only break something!" Just like her mother.

His foot slipped. She heard a rock rattle down the cliffs, and the faint splash as it hit the sea. Bony was still there. Quickly and silently she climbed down to him. He was standing on a narrow ridge, his eyes still shut.

She wanted to tell him to open them and look. To say, "You've done the only tricky bit. It's easy now, as easy as walking upstairs." But she kept silent. She did not think he knew she was there beside him. And he was moving upward again. He was doing all right by himself, the fat tortoise.

Side by side they climbed, up and up. Only when his fingers reached out and touched grass did she nip quickly past him, grab his wrist, and pull him safely over the edge.

He collapsed facedown on the short turf, his head turned away from her. He was trembling violently.

She looked away, not wanting to be caught watching him. Then she leapt to her feet. "I can't see him! He's jumped!" she cried in horror. Then her face relaxed. "Oh, there he is. He's gone back over the fence. . . . He's sitting down and eating his sandwiches!" she exclaimed indignantly, and burst into tears.

Bony led her away from the edge of the cliff toward the fence, patting her shoulder awkwardly. He looked bewildered. "Why are you crying now that it's all over?" he asked, peering at her intently, as if he were trying to see right into her head. She did not tell him.

The weather had changed while they climbed. A mist was rolling toward them from Gullington, lying whitely in the hollows and dimming the sunlight. They walked up the cliff path in silence until they reached the top.

There, sitting in the last patch of sunlight and looking very comfortable, was Mr. Ross.

"Hullo," he said, smiling at them. "I've saved you a sandwich each. I hoped you would come. But I didn't expect you to get here so quickly. How did you do it?"

"We came up the cliffs back there," Felicity said.

"The cliff! But—but wasn't that terribly dangerous?"

Felicity shrugged. "It wasn't too bad. Quite easy, really. Wasn't it, Bony?"

She met his eyes innocently, and Bony looked uncertain. He did not say anything.

"You are brave," Mr. Ross said. He was looking straight at Bony, and it was impossible to believe he did not mean what he said. There was no hint of mockery in his voice. His clear, bright eyes were serious.

Bony flushed. "I wasn't," he muttered. "I'm not brave at all."

"You must be," Mr. Ross said gently. "After all, you're up here now."

Bony stared at him, his face brightening as he realized it was true. He *had* reached the top. He'd done it all by himself, in spite of everything.

Felicity, seeing his smile of pride and pleasure, sighed with relief. Bony'd be all right now. He could go back to being sensible again in peace.

She turned to Mr. Ross. "What did you climb the fence for? Can't you see it's dangerous? Look, you could've been fined fifty pounds!"

"I thought I heard voices," he said apologetically. "I hoped it might be you two. I didn't want to leave without saying good-bye."

"Leave! What do you mean?" Then she noticed the canvas bag on the grass beside him. "You're not going?"

"Yes. I must."

"But you can't go! You can't! What will you do?" Felicity asked in distress. "You haven't any money. Please, come back. Please, Mr. Ross. Mum and Dad said you could stay. Mum was going to let you have one of the vacant guest rooms."

"I know. She told me," Mr. Ross said. "You are all so

kind. I've been very happy here. But it's time I was moving on. I never like to stay in one place too long. I get restless. I am a traveler, you see. Don't worry about me. I have money enough for my needs. Your father insisted on giving me some. And this bag. Your mother agreed," he added with a slight smile.

"She didn't turn you out?" Felicity asked anxiously.

"No. No, indeed. In fact, they both asked me to stay. They were very kind. But I must be going."

"It's not because—because I told on you. About India—"

"India!" he said, and, to her surprise, threw back his head and laughed. "I did enjoy that. Do you remember those books? The temples and the river . . . We put up a good show, didn't we?"

"Books?" Bony asked suspiciously.

"It was just a game we were playing," Mr. Ross said, smiling at Felicity. His eyes were as round and bright as a bird's. She felt they saw everything.

"Who are you?" she asked, staring at him.

"My name is Albert Ross," he said. "I'm quite harmless. Have a sandwich?"

She shook her head. "Don't go," she pleaded. "Don't go yet. Stay a little longer, Mr. Ross."

"I'm afraid I must go," he said, standing up and brushing the crumbs off his trousers. "Are you sure you won't have a sandwich? What about you, Bony? No? Then I might as well take them with me. Good-bye. Good-bye."

He smiled at them, lifted his hand in farewell, and walked quickly away. The misty sunlight glinted for a moment on his pale hair, and a flock of gulls swooped down, whirling and dancing round his head. Then the white mist came up to meet him and he was gone.

They stared after him in silence.

"Weird," Bony said at last. He sounded shaken.

"Where do you think he's going?"

"I don't know." He shrugged. "That's the way to Gullington."

They turned and began walking slowly down the path toward Gull Bay. With every step they took, the extraordinary impression the man had made on them began to fade.

"I suppose he was some sort of joker," Bony said at last. "An out-of-work actor, seeing the chance of a free holiday."

"Mmm."

"Not a bird, anyway. Or a spirit or anything silly like that," he said, looking at her sternly.

"No wings," she agreed meekly. But for a moment she saw, quite clearly, a great silver bird high above the world, its wings now catching the light, now dark against the sun. The wanderer, continuing his journey . . . Then the west wind blew, the sky was covered with a luminous haze, and there was nothing to see.

Felicity was suddenly very happy. Nothing terrible would happen now. The harmless albatross had flown away of its own free will, unhurt. Everything was all right. She and Bony were friends again. Dad would get that job, and Mum could stop worrying about money. Susan had a new boyfriend. Mr. Ross, whatever he might be, had brought them luck.

"I'll tell you one thing," Bony said. "He's not simple. No, he's quite clever, in fact. Understands things."

She looked at him and noticed that his head was higher than it used to be. He was growing. Perhaps one day he'd be as tall as she was. Dad always said boys shot up later. *Why, I needn't have worried*, she thought. *I've got a boyfriend already.*

The idea struck her as so funny that she couldn't resist sharing the joke with Bony, and she burst out laughing at his squeal of dismay. They went running and whooping down the path together, and the pale mist blew around them, turning the gorse bushes into strange, fantastic shapes, like the dreams of childhood.

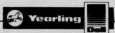

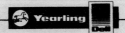
Blairsville High School Library